Girl
OUT LOUD

Girl OUT LOUD

* * * * * * * * * *

EMILY GALE

 SCHOLASTIC INC. / NEW YORK

First published in the United Kingdom in 2010 as *Girl, Aloud*
by Chicken House, 2 Palmer Street, Frome, Somerset BA11 1DS.
www.doublecluck.com

This novel is a work of fiction. Names, characters, places, and incidents are used fictitiously.
Of course the characters in this book only hear Simon Cowell as an imaginary voice in their heads.
We are not quoting from any actual TV shows or real dialogue. "Other Side of the World" lyrics
by KT Tunstall and Martin Terefe © 2004. Produced by Steve Osborne, and released by
KT Tunstall in May 2005 as the second single from her debut album *Eye to the Telescope*
© Relentless Records, 2004.

Library of Congress Cataloging-in-Publication Data
Gale, Emily. [Girl, aloud] Girl out loud / Emily Gale.—1st American ed.
p. cm. "First published in the United Kingdom in 2010 as *Girl, Aloud* by
Chicken House"—Copyright p.
Summary: Fifteen-year-old Kass is trying to resist her manic-depressive father's attempts to make
her try out for *The X Factor* while she also deals with her crush on the same older boy her best
friend likes, her distant mother's mysterious comings and goings, and her younger brother's criminal
activities.

ISBN 978-0-545-30438-2
[1. Family problems — Fiction. 2. Manic-depressive illness — Fiction. 3. Mental illness — Fiction.
4. Friendship — Fiction. 5. Dating (Social customs) — Fiction. 6. England — Fiction.] I. Title.
PZ7.G1313Gi 2012   [Fic]—dc23   2011032710

10 9 8 7 6 5 4 3 2 1   12 13 14 15 16

Printed in the U.S.A.   23
First American edition, June 2012
The text type was set in Adobe Caslon Pro. The display type was set in Century Gothic.
Interior book design by Kristina Iulo

To Madeleine and Jonah,
who are much better
at waiting than I am.

✳ *Chapter One* ✳

A Game Show Host Ate My Dad

Who wants to be . . . a million miles away?

I do.

[Drumroll]

Ladies and Gentlemen, it's Saturday night! Time to play . . .
              Who Wants to Be a *Millionmilesaway?*
And here is your host . . . My Dad!

[Weak applause]

Thank you, thank you, thank you. Yes, I'm Her Dad. Welcome to a
very special edition of . . .
              Who Wants to Be a *Millionmilesaway?*
Let's get right to the first question. Contestant number one, for one

hundred miles: What is this model family of four having for dinner tonight?

For a brief but precious moment I forget that I know the answer—*all* the answers, in fact—to all the questions in the very disturbing pretend game show that goes on in my head when real life gets too tragic. With parents like mine, we're on air pretty much every day.

The answer to the pretend question for a pretend one hundred miles is on the small round table that the contestants are sitting at (the game show host is standing by the oven): four plates, four glasses, four white paper napkins, no knives or forks.

Imaginary Contestant Me: Umm, I'm gonna go with C: Pizza. Pepperoni and mushroom, times two, reheating in the oven against the advice on the box—but I can tell you now that nothing bad happens if you eat reheated pizza, because we do it every Saturday night. Without fail. And we're all still here. Unfortunately.

Game Show Host Dad: It IS pizza! You're on your way to being a millionmilesaway!

Imaginary Contestant Me: I wish. Can we just eat now?

Game Show Host Dad: All in good time! Second question, for two hundred miles: What's for dessert?

The set of *Who Wants to Be a Millionmilesaway?* looks a lot like an eat-in kitchen; the host even wears oven gloves—*The* 'Ove' Glove, to be exact, "as seen on TV," of course. We film on location at 127 Mallow Lane, too far from the city, right on the border of deepest, darkest, dorkiest suburbia.

It's so pristine in here that Ikea could photograph it for their catalog. The lighting is on the slightly painful side of bright, because the game show host likes to see what he's eating. (Living under a flight path as we do, I think we can assume that there are people on planes who can see what we're eating.)

The round table is protected by a vinyl tablecloth with a red apple pattern. The apples are all identical, and shiny, and the kind of vivid red that is probably supposed to make you feel like skipping through an orchard. I once used a black marker to draw a little worm peeking out of one of them, but Mom (aka Contestant Number Two) killed him with one swipe of extra-strength Mr. Clean.

One of the apples hanging down the side has a massive cigarette burn in it. *That* wasn't me.

Game Show Host Dad: I'm going to have to press you for an answer here.

Imaginary Contestant Me: Hmm, that's a toughie. Could it possibly be A: Your homemade pineapple upside-down cake, famous for its chewiness, as in, like a mattress?

Game Show Host Dad: Is that your final answer? You could ask the audience.

Imaginary Contestant Me: Audience? No one watches this show. It's all in my head. The answer is A.

Game Show Host Dad: Right again! You've won TWO hundred miles AND this delicious reheated slice of pizza! Next question, for four hundred: What does this family do after dessert?

The game show host takes a seat next to me—grinning and fidgeting, oblivious to the bright orange pepperoni juice smeared across his cheek. The other contestants chew like robots. In fact there's more going on *underneath* the table.

The legs swinging opposite mine, not close enough to be called kicking but near enough to create a rhythmical wind that scuffs my jeans, belong to Contestant Number Three: my brother, Raff. He is a small-time criminal, a master of deception. On his lap is a BlackBerry. Dad's current favorite gag is to call it a Plum. Last week it was a Strawberry. Can you see where this is going? How many fruits are there in the world? That's how far he'll take it.

The grubby fingers that are not above the table holding reheated pizza are typing speedily but silently. This is one of Raff's many talents that go unnoticed, along with lock picking, pickpocketing, shoplifting, eBaying stolen goods, and credit card fraud. He is thirteen.

The legs to my right are perfectly still; the feet look glued together at the ankles, in shoes I haven't seen before—black with a small heel. Slim legs in beige stockings; the skirt comes just to the knee. This is Contestant Number Two: Grace. My mom.

Strange how, to everyone else, she was Grace before she was Mom, but to me it seems the other way around.

You can't be named Grace and just get away with it; people expect things of you—grace, for a start, and with that a soothing voice, a light touch, a delicate beauty . . . an immaculate Mr. Clean-ed kitchen, smooth hands with manicured nails that never get pizza topping stuck underneath them, quietness, shiny hair, the kind of face that makes you sigh and immediately catch sight of your own, much larger, nose. All that may seem like a huge burden for a one-syllable name, but it's true. And this particular Grace hits all the marks.

The legs to my left can't stop moving. One foot shuffles, the other taps, completely out of time with each other. They stop and the movement travels up the legs, making them jiggle. Stop. Shuffle-tap-jiggle. Stop. Shuffle-tap-jiggle. The legs are hyper. They wear new jeans, trendy ones; the feet are in Nike sneakers, so fresh from the box you could get high off the smell of rubber. If you had to age the legs, you'd say they were in their twenties. Why can't they just be normal like other dads' legs?

He's so twitchy today it's possible he'll spontaneously combust, but I suspect this strangeness is going to lead to something much more damaging. *For me.* It always does when he's like this.

That just leaves my legs—they're on the chubby side of ordinary, and fifteen years old. There is nothing else to say about them.

Imaginary Contestant Me: The answer's B: Play Pictionary.

Game Show Host Dad: You're sure? Remember, you can phone a friend!

Imaginary Contestant Me: My two best friends are at the movies together having a nice time like normal teenagers do on a Saturday night.

Game Show Host Dad: You'll thank me in years to come for this quality family time—it's healthy!

Imaginary Contestant Me: It's killing me.

Game Show Host Dad: Ha-ha! Come on, now, I'm supposed to tell the jokes! OK, for a thousand miles: What's going to happen next?

So this is us; this is how we are. In a second, Dad will jump up and collect the plates, sprint to the kitchen, and put them in the oven. He won't eat reheated pizza off cold plates, so between slices he reheats the plates along with the pizza and we all sit there with nothing to do but *ting* our nails against the glass water pitcher (Mom), type more quietly than the hum of the fridge (Raff), and wait for the rapid-fire round of questions (me).

"How was school?"

"Fine."

"Any tests?"

"No."

"They don't test enough these days. Any essays back?"

"No."

"What's wrong with these teachers?"

Shrug

"Don't worry, Kassidy. Dad's got your future all mapped out."

I hate it when he refers to himself in the third person. But for a rapid-fire round, that was really tame. He's not letting anything get to him tonight—this is what it's always like on his first day back. Back from where? The simple answer would range from "bed" to "armchair" to "bathroom." Those are the only places you'll find him when he's not being one of the two other Dads he's got in him: Vaguely Normal and On The Up, as he calls it, as if that's a good thing. It's basically a frying pan or fire situation.

"Kassidy-Kassidy-Kassidy," he says, using a different facial expression each time he says it, the way you might do *in private* when you're testing out how to say *hi* to a cute boy. "Kassidy Kennedy." He traces imaginary words in the air and looks deep into la-la land. "Oh, yes, oh, *yes*, you're in safe hands, my love."

Great. One of those safe hands is now reaching into the back pocket of the trendy jeans. It pulls out a packet of Marlboros, the strong kind. Unfiltered.

"Just enough time for a quick one before the next batch!" He winks at Mom, she smiles serenely, Raff smiles sarcastically, and I lay my head on the plastic apples and sigh. We all watch him exit the patio doors with his toothy theatrical grin. You'd think living with a person that excitable would whip everyone else up, but when he's like this I just feel dragged down.

Mom clears her throat and tells Raff to eat his crusts. Raff ignores her and types two-handed.

"Can we watch *X Factor*?" I say.

"Well . . ."

"It's on in five minutes."

"No, then. You know Dad likes us to sit together on Saturday evenings. And this is the first day he's been . . ." She doesn't have to say it. *Back.* She means his mind, obviously.

"But it's the finale."

She gets up and goes toward the oven. Thanks as usual, Mom.

"Not yet!" says Dad, and he's in and across the room like a gazelle. He hops a bit from foot to foot in front of the oven door, rubbing his hands, and Mom returns to her seat. Raff's still typing without looking, though he now puts one hand on the table.

"Just stop it," I whisper at Raff as the wind scuff against my jeans becomes too much to bear.

"Stop what?" he whispers back, flapping his legs even harder. I move my chair back a little, hoping that my restraint will annoy him in some small way. I feel like doing something — anything — to stop this from being the dire Saturday night game show it's destined to be, just so I don't know what's going to happen before it does, just so I can't guess every thought in every person's head (except Dad's, which could benefit from some professional headshrinking, let's face it) or every reaction to every single predictable word spoken.

And then Dad does it for me.

"Let's take our seconds into to the other room," he says, and all three of us turn our heads toward him with the kind of speed that could cause whiplash.

"Huh?" says Raff. He has actually stopped typing.

"Excuse me?" says Mom.

I just stare openmouthed at the figure of my father edging toward the kitchen door under the weight of four reheated plates and two reheated pizza boxes.

"I want us to watch *X Factor*," he says, as if that's a perfectly normal thing to announce after years, literally *years*, of us never being allowed to watch Saturday night television for fear of ruining the tradition of the four of us — including whichever version of Dad happens to be present — eating reheated pizza around the round table in our kitchen.

Nobody speaks. Until I do.

"*Why?*" I say, doing nothing to hide my deep suspicion. Dad smiles, the kind of smile that lets me know that there is much, much more to this than I want to know. He doesn't break traditions for nothing.

"They'll be starting a new season of *X Factor* soon," says Dad.

Oh.

God.

No.

"And guess who *I* think should be front and center at the auditions!" It's not a question. He disappears with his load as my chest begins to thud so loudly I'm sure I'm having some sort of heart attack. He's come back from The Dead to deliver my invitation to Personal Hell. Mom gives me a sympathetic look and touches my arm lightly as she says, "Well, you did say you wanted to watch it this evening."

"Yeah, you did say that, Kass." Raff is loving every minute of this. He's even put his BlackBerry away.

"I wanted to watch it, not be ON it," I say, practically hissing. This is serious. This is big. Dad's finally lost it, and he's taking me with him.

Game show over: OFF AIR.

✳ *Chapter Two* ✳

Dad Digs a Really Big Hole, and I Jump In

I lurk in the doorway while the rest of them get comfortable. Dad leaps in front of the TV like a paunchy ballet dancer, remote in hand. He turns the television on but presses the MUTE button, and then he announces:

"I've been thinking."

Here we go. My dad + thinking = very bad thing. In the past, my dad + thinking has equaled:

* *Kassidy should join Mensa!* (international high IQ society)
* *Kassidy is entering a chess tournament!*
* *I've signed Kassidy with a child modeling agency!*
* *Kassidy* must *try out for the National Youth Orchestra!*

And now watch him transform from wonderful, supportive parent to deranged, embarrassing idiot when we look at the rest of the facts:

11

* *Kassidy's IQ is so low that . . . she doesn't even know what IQ stands for.*
* *Kassidy only remembers the name of one chess piece. A prawn, isn't it?*
* *Anyone can sign with this child modeling agency (for $500).*
* *Kassidy barely managed "Twinkle, Twinkle, Little Star" on beginner's violin. Even then, she suspects, her dad bribed the teacher to keep her in the holiday assembly — in the back row, behind the tuba section.*

(I hate it when I think about myself in the third person.)

But I could go on. When I say it doesn't take much to get Dad "thinking," I mean that I've become so self-conscious about my "talents" that I've even developed an unattractive walk. Seriously. He will pick up on anything when he's On The Up.

"What the audience of this show *loves* is the Wild Card. The Underdog. The one who starts off at the bottom but somehow steals our hearts." He doesn't just *say* these words, he *performs* them. It's nauseating.

"And," he whispers, looking from Mom to Raff and then to me, "her voice isn't half bad, either!"

I quickly rewind back over the past few days until I remember Dad clapping like a seal in my bedroom doorway, where he'd obviously been standing for some time to watch me applying mascara while singing something (out of tune) from my old KT Tunstall playlist. That was the spark. *THAT.* It's like watching me brush my teeth and telling me I should be a dentist.

I can't sing.

I canNOT sing.

Glued to the door frame, I am still taking all of this in. I've been here before and it hasn't ended well, for anyone. I don't want to say a single word until I am sure my words will be convincing enough, but all I can think of so far is:

Help!

I want my insanely dull Saturday night back; I promise never to complain about reheated pizza and pineapple upside-down cake again.

"*You've* got the likability factor, Kassidy," says Dad.

"The *what*?" says Raff.

"It's what Simon says. Likability. It's even more important than having a good voice — and Kassidy has *got* it."

My brother comes over to me.

"*This* Kassidy?" he says. "Uh, she only has *two* friends. How is she likable?"

He's right, but I'd still like to hit him.

"Raff, if you've got nothing helpful to contribute . . ." Dad wags his remote with a stern look on his face, and Raff takes a seat with his hands in a prayer position as if we've just been doing judo, an impish grin on his face.

Mom is doing her nervous throat-clearing thing. As usual, she's choosing to ignore what's going on. Well, it's not as if Dad's On The Up mood affects *her*.

Dad unmutes the TV, and he and Raff chew pizza and grin at each other like happy pigs eating from a trough. My dad is too dense to realize that Raff is laughing *at* him, not with him. Raff knows that when Dad is occupied with a grand plan for me, the spotlight isn't going anywhere near him for a long time, and that can only mean: *ka-ching*!

Mom pats a space next to her to beckon me in.

"Come on, it's just the commercials now," she says. But as I sink into fake leather, I see I've been duped.

"If YOU want to audition for the next season of The X Factor, *here's what you need to know."*

My dad knees his way toward the television with half a slice of pizza in his mouth and a pad and pen in his hands.

"What are you writing, Dad?"

He's scribbling so hard the paper rips every now and then, and he flips over to the next page, filling the space with wild sketches and his huge, loopy handwriting.

"Ideas for song choices, the kind of look you should go for, the rules of entry—everything, Kassidy! I'm totally on top of this. You don't have to worry about a thing."

I've never seen anyone break into a sweat just from writing fast—since when does penmanship count as cardio? But the man is unstoppable.

Then suddenly a list of rules pops up on the TV screen and one of them catches my eye.

"Wait, look!" My voice is so excited I sound like I've inhaled a helium balloon. "'Contestants may not have a current contract relating to the use of their voice or likeness,'" I read off the screen. "Says it right there, Dad: I'm not eligible! Fish sticks, everyone! FISH STICKS!!" Butt-bouncing on the sofa and punching the air is probably not a good look, but I'm oh so very happy. So. Very. HAPPY! The horror is over before it's begun. I'm saved. By a frozen fish product.

The worst audition of my life just so happened to end in a commercial for Gorton's, and I've been carrying the shame of advertising ground-up bits of fish in a crispy coating ever since, but now . . . they're a total lifesaver!

Picture me in the churning ocean gripping tight to a giant frozen stick of fish as I ride on its crumbly orange back to the safety of the shore! Sticks ahoy!

But wait, why is Dad shaking his head, revealing a smug smile oozing with pizza?

"Dad? Stop with that look. No way around it, I'm the fish sticks girl!" Never said it with *that* level of enthusiasm before. "We can't break the Gorton's contract; it would be illegal!"

"Pshaw! Minor technicality," he says, with a flourish of his pen on yet another new sheet of paper. "Consider it dealt with."

SOS: The Good Ship Fish Stick has sprung a leak.

"You can't be serious! So now you're turning me into a criminal? What if they sue me? No way."

"Yes, way."

How can I debate reasonably with a thirty-nine-year-old who still uses the no-way/yes-way tactic? I need new ideas, and fast.

"Dad, think about it—people always get caught when they

lie about things on these shows. We could ruin my future in showbiz for good." (Pause for a second as I let myself think how great that would actually feel.) "Why not just wait a year or two until the Gorton's contract runs out?"

He's quiet for a moment — *Stop the Presses, People, He's Actually Thinking About It!* "Plus, Dad, look at me — I still look way more fish sticks than pop star."

Raff comes over, snarling in the direction of my chest. "'S true. She's got no boobs, look."

I gasp and cross my arms over my chest, and try unsuccessfully to punch him in the head with my elbow. Dad roars: "Rafferty! Stop looking at your sister and go have another slice of pizza."

I hate to agree with my brother — ever — but he has a point. Plus I know how much my dad hates talking about things like "boobs." I might be able to embarrass him into submission.

"Raff's right, Dad. They're flatter than fried eggs."

"That has nothing to do with . . . anything," he says. "No more talk of . . . them. I've got to think about this Gorton's thing."

"You've done enough thinking," I mumble. He takes another huge bite of pizza.

"I've got it," I think he says, though it's slightly muffled until he swallows. "We'll say the fish-sticks girl wasn't you; it was your cousin, who died!"

"Paul!" Mom hardly ever "Pauls" him. At least it's not just me who thinks he's finally lost his one remaining marble. I only *have* one cousin, and I'm pretty fond of her!

"That's not *getting* it," I say. "That's the opposite of getting it.

16

I'm not eligible *and* I'm tone-deaf, Dad. Game over. The End. Let's just turn it off and play Pictionary." (You know things are desperate in this house when someone volunteers to play a competitive game with Dad in the room. Especially Pictionary. Especially when he's like this. We could end up with extravagant doodles all over the wallpaper, like the ghost of Keith Haring on a caffeine high.)

"This is your twist," he says. "Everyone needs a twist on this show — a gimmick, something people will remember, something *moving*. A dead cousin, spitting image of you — who *wouldn't* shed a tear about that? I couldn't expect a true star like you to degrade herself with fish sticks!" Dad gets up and paces the room as if he's solving a crime. As a matter of fact, this *is* a crime, with several charges: violating a contract, entering a competition under false pretenses, and child cruelty, for starters. But Dad will never point the (fish) finger at himself.

"Dad, people will remember me for being an *epic fail*. You know this — every time we end up at that Japanese restaurant for somebody's birthday you beg me to sing karaoke, and I never, *ever* fail to suck!"

He is chewing pizza so quickly it's made him profoundly deaf. I try again.

"Anyway, saying I have a dead cousin isn't a twist, it's a lie."

"It's terrible," says Mom, too quietly to have any effect.

"It's brilliant! Your likability and my sales skills . . . come on, you guys, you know I could sell Ben & Jerry's to Victoria Beckham! I'm On The Up!!"

Affirmative. He's in another world. And I'm in hell. Suddenly he jabs his pepperoni slice in my direction.

"Sing us something, Kassidy. Come on, just a few bars." He tries to get me up and over to the mantelpiece using bare enthusiasm, as if I'm some dumb pug in a Doritos commercial. "She's good, Grace, she's really improved." My mom smiles at him. *Don't* smile at him, Mom; that'll just encourage him! "This is it," he says, clenching his fist as if he's just discovered a way of turning house dust into gold.

He's too far gone now for me to argue. It could make him worse. My dad's not like other people. I feel awful saying that. It's not that I've completely forgotten all the ways that he can be amazing like other dads don't seem to be—like the spur-of-the-moment trip to Disney World, or the day he got his ear pierced with me because I was scared to do it on my own—but lately it feels like he needs HANDLE WITH CARE tattooed on his forehead.

I need help, and I'm not going to get it in this room. If I protest any more he'll list every sales job he's ever had and every dream sale he ever made, starting with the legendary Lil' Paul's Lemonade Stand (circa 1983) and not forgetting the time he unloaded three washing machines on the same desperate house-wife (well, *I'd* buy three washing machines just to make him *GO AWAY!*). Or Worse. And believe me, there is a Worse. It's not the kind of Worse you can get locked up for, but it's the kind you don't invite to parties. It's the kind nobody really talks about.

I've got to get out of here.

"Actually, Dad, I've got a bit of a tickle in my throat. Better save my voice, don't you think?"

From the look on his face you'd think I said *terminal*, not *tickle*. He clamps my shoulders meaningfully between his hands and looks into my eyes. Then he runs from the room and the rest of us wait in limbo. When he returns it is with a glass of cloudy liquid, which he stirs frantically, not noticing the small spills on his running shoes.

"Here, drink this."

"What is it?"

"Salt water. The professionals use it."

I look at Raff, who cannot conceal his joy.

"That's right," Raff says. "Britney uses it."

Dad snatches the glass from my hand.

"But she's ruined herself," he says to Raff. "Two young children and all that rehab for that, umm, whatever it is she's got." We all go deathly silent, and there's only the sound of the spoon clinking around the glass. He looks at the drink as if salt water were directly responsible for Britney's downfall.

Raff nods and says, "True, but I also heard that Adele drinks it."

"Really?" Dad's face lights up again. He stops stirring and passes the drink back. The temptation to throw it over my brother is huge—he doesn't have to put up with any of this unwanted attention, and all he can do is gloat—but I've got to play the long game here. This is no time for rash actions.

I cough a little and put my hand to my throat as if I'm in pain. It's lame, but it works.

"I'd better take this upstairs and then get some rest."

"Yes, yes, off you go, Kassidy." As I'm walking away he's saying, "Good name for a pop star, isn't it?" And Raff is agreeing and Mom is silent, of course.

I trudge up to my refuge with a glass of spew. Dad's still bouncing around and I can barely put one foot in front of the other. How can someone being that happy make me feel this bad? But here's the irony. This is how we *all* prefer Dad — just barely — because when he's not acting like this, he's being something completely different, and you really, really don't want to know.

The decision of whether to call Izzy or Char is made for me when I look at the time: nine thirty. There are probably all sorts of reasons I don't know about why the children of divorced parents are allowed to take calls later, but the rule hasn't made it to Char's house (probably because her dad is still massively in denial about her mom walking out). So I'm dialing Izzy even though I'm more in the mood for Char (but definitely not in the mood for Char's dad giving me a lecture on the polite time to use the telephone). Besides, Char seemed a bit stressed out last week, which isn't like her, so she probably doesn't need me dumping a whole bunch of anxiety on her shoulders. By contrast, Izzy will ask for seconds. She's an issues junkie.

There are good points and bad points to knowing someone as

long as I've known Izzy. BAD: She knows all the really embarrassing stuff that's happened to me. GOOD: She knows all the really embarrassing stuff that's happened to me, and she's *still* hanging around. But sometimes I wish I could have kept it all to myself, kept the conversation about normal things, like GTL on *Jersey Shore* instead of GTDs in my house: that's Dad's Gray Tracksuit Days, which usually turn into Gray Tracksuit Weeks, and recently even into Gray Tracksuit Month, which, at the end of last year, was about the worst thing that's ever happened to this family. It coincided with Dad finding out that I'd secretly resigned from the debate team at school, and a big fight we had about my future. Mom must have said, "It's not your fault," about a hundred times. She's a terrible liar.

The trouble is that while the GTDs happen behind closed doors, when Dad's On The Up even carbon-steel-armored doors with patented locking systems couldn't contain him (don't ask how I know about those). He's truly Out There.

Because my night/life is already ruined, I'm not surprised at all when it's Izzy's mom who answers the phone. She's a therapist. The therapist is in therapy. The therapist's daughter is in therapy. The therapist's ex is a lawyer, and he's not in therapy, but the therapist and the therapist's daughter, who are in therapy, think he should be. Talking to Izzy about her family is guaranteed to give me either a headache or a lisp.

"Hi there, Kass. How are you feeling?" The way she says *feeeeling* is clearly meant to be very *soooothing*.

"Really great, thanks, Mrs. Franklin—I mean, *Doctor*

Franklin!" I try to sound like I've just slid off a rainbow, happy happy joy joy, so that she doesn't ask me to lie down on her imaginary couch.

"It's Barbara, darling, please." (I know it is, and we've had this conversation about once a week since I was little.)

"OK, sorry, Barbara! May I—"

"Are you sure you're all right, Kass? You sound a bit—"

"No, I'm *really* great, thanks. *Barbara.*"

"How's school, then? Izzy never tells me anything."

I am *really* tempted to suggest that Izzy's mom should ask Izzy's therapist how school is, as Izzy readily admits she tells her therapist *everything*.

"It's really great." I know I sound as if the rainbow high has worn off a bit, but I'm too exasperated to bother now. *I don't want to speak to you, Barbara! Please put your daughter on, Barbara!*

"And how's the family?"

"Fine. Really fine. Is Izzy back from the movies, *please?*" Great, now I sound like the rainbow ride has turned my stomach and I'm desperately looking around for somewhere to vom.

"I'll just get her." She sounds really put out that I didn't want to chat more. Yuck. I feel bad enough when I upset my own parents, let alone someone else's.

"Hi, it's me. What's up, Furbs?" Izzy sounds very grown-up and serious, although she's still managing to call me by the pet name I loathe beyond all loathing (I may have neglected to tell *her* this). *Apparently* I used to look like a Furby. It was a long time ago: My hair now covers my ears.

"It's my dad."

"Oh. I saw him earlier. He had tons of shopping bags."

"Yeah, he went out and bought all these clothes he's way too old for."

"Oh, *God*. My dad did that when he turned forty, except he bought a Porsche and went out with a teenage stripper."

"Izzy, she was in her late twenties and she worked at the Carphone Warehouse."

"Yeah, well, whatever. Count yourself lucky."

"Sure, remind me to count myself lucky when I'm standing in a mile-long line waiting to SING in front of SIMON COWELL."

"What?"

"That's what he wants me to do."

"Who? Simon Cowell?"

"My dad!"

"Oh. But, Furbs, you can't really sing—not to be harsh or anything. You can do lots of other things."

"I know I can't sing, Izz. You don't have to tell me that." Hearing her say it does sting a little, even though I know she's right. I stop speaking for a moment to give her room to list the things I *can* do. . . .

Izz? Got any examples?

Silence.

I almost wish I'd risked it and called Char instead. She spins sympathy like a spider spins silk. She'll wrap you in it like a cocoon, and even though you know you can't stay in there forever, it feels really good while you do. Izzy's into realism and cold, hard truths.

"You're under contract! Simple. He's not going to go as far as breaking the rules," she says.

"He's going as far as breaking the law, Izz. As in breaking the fish-stick deal. And killing off a nonexistent cousin."

She gasps. "Seriously?"

"Yes—I never thought I'd make it to juvenile prison before my brother."

"Well, just say *no*, then." Sometimes, as a trainee therapist, she can be very simplistic.

"You *know* that doesn't work on my dad."

"So he's still having those episodes?"

"What 'episodes'?" I can hear the extra harshness in my voice, and my heart is beating really loud now that Izzy has said that. *Episodes? It's not* Gossip Girl. *It's my dad.*

"Don't get stressed, I just mean that your dad has some undiagnosed . . . well, *I* know the term for it but you don't like to talk about it, so . . . Come to think of it, doesn't he always buy a whole bunch of new clothes when he starts a new cycle?"

"Oh, does he? Well, thanks, Doctor, I'll pass that on." I don't want to feel this mad with Izzy but I can't help it when she gets like this. *I'm* allowed to talk like that about Dad, but it hurts too much when she does. As soon as anyone else is mean about him it unlocks the musty old room in my brain that stores all the good stuff about Dad.

Half of me knows that Izzy is still talking, but the other half is remembering the summer I turned twelve. It was the day before a new school year and we'd spent all of August away—Dad had sprung it on us. He'd picked up Mom from work, Raff from day camp, and then me. "Get in! We're going to Disney World!" I can remember the looks of amazement on Izzy's and Char's faces as we drove away with Dad still shouting about our plans through the car window. *His* plans. He'd packed all our stuff; no questions asked, he'd thought of everything. It was like being in a movie—a whole month of the Magic Kingdom and SeaWorld, twenty-four-hour room service and the hotel pool. Unreal.

But then we were back home and I'd confessed that there was an important school project due the next morning. It was supposed to be about "Some Everyday Thing That We Don't Know Much About." I'd let myself forget all about it, but now I felt sick with how stupid I'd been and couldn't face going to school empty-handed.

"You can still do it, Kassidy," said Dad.

"Dad, don't be ridiculous," I said. "There are only twelve hours between now and school, and I don't even know what the project is going to be about!"

Mom had been hovering in the kitchen doorway.

"Cookies and milk, anyone?" she said.

"Excellent!" said Dad, jumping up. It was the most over-the-top response to an offer of cookies anyone had ever seen.

"It's just a snack, Dad," I said.

"Ah, but it's not, is it? It's your project, Kassidy! Some Everyday

Thing That We Don't Know Much About. COOKIES! Come on, we can do this."

"We?" I said.

But he was already flicking through his phone book, muttering something about a guy who worked for Keebler owing him a favor, and before I knew it the living room had been transformed into Operation Help Kassidy — and by seven o'clock in the morning (hours after I'd fallen asleep with a pen in my hand) I had the weirdest and most amazing project on cookies ready to hand in — complete with home-baked chocolate chips (ahoy?) for the whole class.

Dad slept for two whole days after that. I can't remember what happened next, which usually means it wasn't good. I only got a B+ but I didn't tell him that.

Now I tune back in to what Izzy's been saying.

"Look, Furbs, he can't actually *make* you audition. It's cruelty to minors. Simon Cowell is the original mean judge — for years they've used him to clone other mean judges."

"Yeah, I know! It'll be a bloodbath. TV's Mr. Nasty meets a tone-deaf banana. But there's nothing I can do."

"You have rights. You're not his puppet."

"Oh, yeah? You do remember the audition, don't you?"

"God, yes. Oh, Furbs. Poor you."

And just like that we're in the other room in my brain — the much bigger room, which is full of all the *other* stuff about Dad.

Picture three children in the hallway of a small Victorian house. The two girls are eight years old (the one who isn't me looks at least ten) and are trying desperately to ignore the boy, who is six and wants to show them his top score on Tetris.

"Just buzz off."

"But look how good I am."

"Daaaaaad, Raff's annoying us, are we going yet?"

The dad springs down the stairs. He is wearing a look that makes one of the girls feel a teensy bit suspicious, though she isn't old enough or jaded enough to recognize this look as "very sheepish."

"Are we going to the zoo now?" she says.

"Everyone in the car!" he says, ushering the three of them out the front door with the cheesy enthusiasm of a game show host.

On the road, the taller, serious-looking girl whispers to the other, "I don't think this is the way to the zoo."

"'Course it is," says the other girl, who sometimes finds her friend a bit of a know-it-all.

Half an hour later the car stops in front of an old theater.

"I told you," whispers the know-it-all friend. The other girl shushes her—she still 80 percent believes that her dad has brought them to the zoo, though this looks nothing like the pictures she's seen on TV.

Inside the theater, the dad speaks to a woman who gives him a number and checks off a box on her clipboard. The dad pins the number on the girl.

"Does this mean I can go in the monkey house?" she asks.

"This way!" says the cheesy game show dad. There's a stage, and on it is a line of children. One by one they go over to a table, at which sits an old man with a gray beard who is dressed in a naval uniform.

"You're late," says a woman with very glitzy glasses and a stern suit and another clipboard. She uses her chin to point violently toward the back of the line onstage, and then she looks at the front of the line and shouts: "NEXT! OK, for the last time the words are: *Trust the Gorton's Fisherman.*"

She is very scary; so scary that the girl's left knee starts to give way when she's walking down the aisle toward the stage, as the dad is pushing her to do. And he's whispering to her. *You just need to say one line . . . just do what they tell you . . . try to be natural . . . smile . . . I just know you're going to do great . . . make your dad proud, OK?*

She is *still* clinging on to the 20 percent of her that thinks the dad has brought her to the zoo. But the percentage begins to fall as she climbs the stairs onto the stage, joins the line of girls, and looks back at the know-it-all friend and the annoying little brother and the beaming dad.

And then she feels dizzy—what was the line again?—and then she feels something warm trickling down her leg and into her sock. She is frozen to the spot, and all she can see is the dad's big cheesy set of teeth. But as the girl next to her starts to nudge her a bit, she sees the smile disappear into his mouth, and she can hear someone saying, *Wet herself,* and all the muscles that were holding up her dad's expression seem to collapse, and then she can hear someone saying, *For God's sake, get her off,* and the dad is holding his hand out but not looking at her, helping her back down the stairs and up the aisle to where the know-it-all friend and the annoying little brother are standing with their mouths wide open and something in their eyes she will later recognize as pity.

Phew. It still makes me nauseous just thinking back to that day. "Trust the Gorton's fisherman." As if! Like I'd wanted to advertise something as corny as that. I didn't want to advertise *anything* (except maybe my need for a new dad).

I cried the whole way home, not just because I'd wet myself in front of dozens of people but also because Izzy had tried to warn me that we weren't really going to the zoo and I hadn't listened to her — I'd even been mad at her for doubting my dad. But most of the tears were for the look on Dad's face. Even after he'd lied to me and humiliated me, *I* still felt like I'd let *him* down. And then, the next week, we got the call: They cast me anyway! I mean, seriously, what does a kid have to do to screw up an audition? (A number two?!?)

Izz breaks into my thoughts. "Are you still there, Furbs?"

"Yeah, sort of," I say.

"I'm sure Mom's got a pamphlet on this in her office."

"No, thanks."

"Hey, do you want my help or not?"

"Not. Not really. I just called you as a friend, not as a shrink."

This always happens. Why do I never learn? I should have kept this private, except it seems to affect so much of my life that if I kept it *all* to myself I'd have nothing to say, ever.

"*Maybe* you really do want free therapy," she says, teasing me.

"*Maybe* the lady doth protest too much, methinks."

"Yeah, well, *me*thinks you should shove that copy of *Hamlet* up your butt." (We're doing it in English Lit—not shoving it, just reading it.) "Anyway, how was the movie?" I change the subject and my tone because it's getting too tense, and Izzy's not helping as much as she'd like to. But I'm grateful, I guess, that she doesn't run screaming in the opposite direction, considering all the weird behavior she's witnessed in this house.

I make sure we have a decent convo about normal things before I tell her I have to go and that I'll call her tomorrow.

Afterward I lie down on my unmade futon and close my eyes.

—*Hello, sweetheart, and what's your name?*

—*It's Kassidy. I mean, Kass, Kass Kennedy. Sorry, Mr. Cowell.*

—*OK, Kass-Kass Kennedy, what makes you think you've got the X Factor?*

—*It's just Kass, Mr. Cowell.*

—*Right. Just Kass. So, what makes you stand out from the rest?*

. . .

—*Anything?*

. . .

—*Anything at all? Come on, sweetheart, we're filming here.*

—*I'm just really ordinary, Mr. Cowell. I'm average.*

—*Great. Fabulous. Just what we're looking for. Right, says here you're eight years old.*

—*No, I'm fifteen.*

—*It says eight here. You must be mistaken. And what are you going to sing for us today?*

—*"Suddenly I See," by KT Tunstall.*

—*Mm. It's not very "young," is it? Do you know any other songs?*

—*No, just that one.*

—*Ugh. OK then, go ahead if you must.*

. . .

—*I said start.*

. . .

—*Darling, if you're not going to sing, you're just wasting my time.*

—*Sorry, I'll do it now.*

—*Fine.*

—*Trust the Gorton's fisherman!*

—*Pardon?*

—*TRUST THE GORTON'S FISHERMAN!*

—*Oh, God, have you just wet yourself? Security, get her out of here, will you?*

—*But listen, I've really got it now:*

> *TRUST THE GORTON'S FISHERMAN!*
> *TRUST THE GORTON'S FISHERMAN!*
> *TRUST THE GORTON'S FISHERMAN!*

✳ *Chapter Three* ✳

He Might As Well Stand at the Front Door with a Sawed-off Shotgun

Sunday mornings should be sacred. I don't mean religious; I mean that I should be able to walk downstairs wearing an old, stained hoodie and track pants and with mascara smudged under my eyes without running into a pervy thirteen-year-old who looks at me as if I'm Chloë Moretz at a premiere.

He's enormous compared to the Miniature Terror I call my brother—the same height as me, how irritating. Since when did Raff's ankle-biting friends hit puberty? This one even has tiny bits of black fluff sprouting from his chin, but it looks more like dirt than stubble. He also has alarmingly pink cheeks and bulging eyes: a sort of giant furry clowny toad. This is typical; no one normal could ever be into me.

"Hey. I'm Lucas. Luke." The voice is like someone's first try on a violin, but it's pretty brave of him to introduce himself. It's as if he's been practicing a tutorial, like the kind people use to learn French. I look at Raff, sitting cross-legged in front

32

of the Wii, but he is oblivious to this revolting attack.

Now the Toad is looking at me as if I'm ice cream. *Shiver* Isn't he on the young side for hormones?

"Hi, Lucas, *Luke*," I say, trying to sound as unappealing as I can by mocking his little intro. Dad comes in from the kitchen, wiping his hands on a dish towel. His outfit + his bounciness = there has been no Return to Planet Earth overnight.

"Good morning, sweetheart. How's the throat? You sound a bit croaky. Didn't the salt water help?" He wipes his hands harder and looks me all over as if he's checking for a rash. The Toad takes this as his cue to come closer and do the same.

"Are you sick, Kass?" says Toady.

"No." I pull my hood up over my head to scowl inside. Who *is* this brat?

"Are you cold?" says Dad, and he goes to put the dish towel around my shoulders.

"No! Can I just sit down?" They both make room for me to get to the sofa and gawk as if any minute I'm going to morph into a rare yellow-tailed woolly monkey and start swinging from the ceiling beams. Finally I'm saved by Raff.

"Luke, are you playing or what?"

The Toad reluctantly joins him.

"What can I get you for breakfast?" says Dad.

"Just coffee, Dad. Thanks."

"Eggs? Oatmeal? Bran flakes? You should have some fiber."

"How is fiber going to make me a better singer?" I already want to cry. I wish I'd never come downstairs.

"OK, OK, I don't want you getting upset. Coffee, then." On his way into the kitchen he passes Mom as if she's a pillar in the way instead of a person; she looks at him, but I can't quite tell what the look is, and smiles an *oh, well* smile at me as she takes a pile of folded towels upstairs. She mouths *Morning*. I scowl; it's not really meant for her but for my general situation.

In my sleepiness I become transfixed on what Raff and Lucas are up to.

"I'll put a dollar on the Cowboys, with an extra dollar for Romo for most completed passes," says Lucas.

"I can give you odds of seven to one for Dallas and three to one for Romo," says Raff, consulting a small red notebook. They are both speaking out of the sides of their mouths in hushed tones and looking around shiftily. This is like watching *Ocean's Eleven — The Early Years*. Lucas nods and they shake hands, clumsily exchanging bills as they do. Raff reaches under his fleece top and pulls out a black drawstring pouch. Who does he think he is now, the Monopoly banker?

"What about the other bet?" says Lucas, bending nearer my brother. Raff catches my eye for an instant.

"Not now, later."

"Um, what's going on?" I say.

"Nothing, Mariah," says Raff.

"You'd better not be betting on me, you little rat-face."

"Don't flatter yourself, Taylor Swiftless."

"Don't be a jerk, Raff," says Lucas. Wonderful: A thirteen-year-old overfizzing with hormones is my only supporter.

"Thanks, Lucas, but I can stick up for myself," I say.

"Sorry, Kass." His wounded-puppy look is no more appealing than his lovesick gaze. "Anyway, Raff, it's just Swift. My mom's got *Fearless*."

"No duh. Who cares?"

"No one. Shut up."

"*You* fucking shut up."

My dad pops his head into the room and for a second I think he's going to call Raff out for swearing, but like all Raff's sins it goes unnoticed and Dad just gives me the thumbs-up sign, bobs around, and pouts with his bottom lip. Then he puts the dish towel over his head and swings it like it's dreadlocks. It's a shame I'm not three years old or he'd have really cheered me up by now.

The doorbell rings.

I wouldn't usually be the first to get up to answer; especially not on a Sunday morning, dressed like a vagrant and still caked in yesterday's face. It barely registers when Lucas says, "That's probably my brother."

"Hi, is this the Kennedys'? I'm Cass."

"Huh?" The weather that comes through the door is cold enough to burn, but that's not what's making me freeze. There is some kind of demigod standing at my door; well, either that or not washing your mascara off at night can profoundly warp your eyesight.

"I said, I'm Cass. I'm Lucas's brother."

"Oh. Hi." Is this how one addresses a demigod, I wonder?

"He's here, isn't he?"

"Yeah, he is, yeah."

There is a pause. A tiny part of me knows that the pause is because I'm checking him out from head to toe, but that tiny part is unfortunately located in a dormant part of my brain.

"Well, I'm here to pick him up," he says, in that sweet, deep way of his. (Already he has "a way.")

Suddenly the door is pulled back behind me.

"Let him in, you idiot," says Raff. "Hi, Cass."

"Oh, sorry!" I say, and giggle, and squeak slightly when the Other Cass catches my little toe with his big brown boots. He didn't mean it, obviously. He just has really, really big boots, and my stupid toe was in the stupid way.

"My name's Kass, too," I say, but my voice seems to have disappeared inside my unwashed, saggy track pants and he doesn't hear over the noise of football cheering.

"What's the score, dudes?" he asks. He crouches down and puts his hands on the bases of their necks affectionately.

"Seven–zip, Cowboys."

"Which one of you is Dallas?"

"Me," says his brother, beaming at the Other Cass. Lucas gets a head ruffle and I feel awful for being so mean to him before. When he's not perving on me, he looks like quite a sweet kid.

I stand there behind the Other Cass and ponder his tousled hair, the color of dark chocolate. Would it be so very wrong to go over and smell it? Suddenly I realize he might be able to see my reflection gawking in the television.

"Did you want a Coke or something?" I say. I think I've

crossed and uncrossed my arms a dozen times since he walked in. I've also made three resolutions:

I am never getting up late again.

I am never going to bed in makeup again.

I am never being mean to dear, sweet Lucas again.

The Other Cass gets up and wanders away from the boys and toward me slightly, sideways, keeping an occasional eye on the screen. What, my just-rolled-out-of-bed look isn't utterly captivating? Amazing.

Dad shouts from the kitchen: "Are you sure you don't want eggs, Kass?"

"I'm sure, Dad," I shout back. The Other Cass looks really confused (and yet still remarkably sexy). "Kass is my name, too," I say. "Well, Kassidy, but only my dad calls me that, I don't actually like it, so I'm just Kass, like you." Somebody switch me off, quick.

"I'm Cassian." He offers his hand, and a knock-you-off-your-feet smile. I just about manage not to giggle when I shake it. I notice how clean his fingernails are, unlike those of most boys I know—most of the boys I know being Raff's friends. (I haven't quite made it to the dating scene I hear so much about—whatever, I've been busy having my entire life ruined by my dad.) But Cass seems about twenty years older than any other boy I've ever spoken to—in a good way. Hand-shaking? Being nice to little brothers? Those enormous brown boots? And don't even get me started on his eyes (green). We've barely spoken and already I'm starting to obsess.

"So, you go to St. Agatha's?" he says.

"Yes, how did you know?"

"Not sure, I think Raff told me." My heart plummets: If Raff talks about me to hand-shaking boys in brown boots, it's almost definite that he knows all my warts already—actual and metaphorical. I have an actual one right now on my elbow. It's *hugely* unlikely that he can see it under the stained hoodie, but I put my hand over it anyway.

"Where do *you* go?" I say, hoping not to sound like a stalker.

"Dudley. Know it?"

Never heard of it. I nod vigorously.

"What are you studying, Cass?" I can't say his name without smiling, and I don't think I've ever been more aware of my teeth. I feel like a very nervous horse.

"A whole bunch of 'ologies," he says. "Nothing interesting." I'd beg to differ, only I've heard the begging look is not that attractive. "Hey, who's the stamping guy I passed on the way here?"

"Oh, that's the Stamping Man," I say, immediately wishing I hadn't announced it as if he were a sideshow attraction.

"So I almost got his name right."

I don't know what to make of this. He's smiling at me but I feel really stupid.

"Um, yeah. Well, he stamps. A lot. For hours, actually, in the same spot. He's done it for years. It's weird because he's really well dressed. But we don't normally walk that way."

The Other Cass kind of nods and smiles, but I'm sure behind that smile he is deeply unimpressed.

"Here we are, Kassidy. Sorry I took so long—burned the first pot while I was checking something out on the Internet for the audition." There's a faint buzzing in my left ear that I really hope is a pesky fly and not my peskier dad.

"Morning, Mr. Kennedy," says the Other Cass.

Damn, so it *is* my dad. And now he's shaking hands with the Other Cass, and all I can think is that I never want these two people to be in the same room together, especially if I'm also in it. While they exchange niceties I edge my way to the staircase. As much as I want to be near Brown Boots for a bit longer, even if he's going to crush my little toe again, I can't take the risk.

"Kass, your coffee!"

Double damn.

"Great, thanks. Mmm, yummy." *Yummy?* Am I five years old, and is this a cup of hot cocoa topped with mini-marshmallows?

"So what's this audition?" says the Other Cass.

"It's nothing," I say with lightning speed, narrowing my eyes at Dad, who is, of course, looking in the opposite direction.

"It's for *The X Factor*," says Dad. The Other Cass laughs, though not in an obviously unkind way.

"Go for it, Mr. Kennedy!"

"Oh, it's not for me; it's Kass here. She's very talented."

"I'm not; I'm *so* not." This is hopeless. "Anyway, nice to meet you. Bye."

It's a terrible idea to leave my dad talking to a hand-shaking hottie in brown boots with the same name as me, but it's on par with having to witness the event. That's settled, then: I will die alone, surrounded by cats.

"See ya. Good luck. Sounds cool," he says.

Ugh. I'm heartbroken already. I haven't even got the strength to turn back around and thank him.

It's at times like this that I remember why I chose the room at the top of the house. Most people focus on the bad points:

1. There is almost no floor space, what with my bed, dresser, desk, and collection of Desperate Dad gifts designed to bring out the high achiever he's convinced is buried underneath my ordinary skin but which have achieved precisely nothing other than a layer of dust over the years (the easel, the electronic keyboard, the cello, the surfboard . . .).
2. There is almost no space above my head in the middle of the room, and the sloping walls mean that I've had to develop a semipermanent stoop.
3. There is almost no light.
4. There is even less air.
5. It is almost certainly a fire hazard.

But I wouldn't change it for the world. Even the constant cooing that seeps through the roof day and night doesn't bother me. I'm sick of everyone picking on pigeons, anyway. When we moved here, Raff thought he'd get one over on me by giving me the nickname Pidge and trying to make it catch on.

"Pidge lives up in the roof. *Cooo-cooo,*" he'd say in a high-pitched birdie voice whenever someone came over. I really didn't mind—suits me better than Kassidy, or even Kass, which I manage to insist on to everyone but Dad—but Dad put a stop to Pidge.

Up here, I can almost forget about down there. Up here, they don't seem *so* bad. Usually. Take Raff (please, someone take Raff)—even he has his good points. Sometimes I lie awake at night and try to remember what they are. Once I came up with: *He has a chicken phobia.* I know that doesn't sound like a good point exactly, but it's a weakness, and believe me, any chink in that boy's armor is something to be cherished.

He was seven or so when he first developed a habit of sneaking frozen food up to his room and sucking on it like Popsicles. It was mainly peas, sometimes sweet corn, but one day he took a chicken breast and devoured the whole thing while playing one-handed Halo. He was so, so sick. The next time Mom served chicken, he made a distressed baboon noise, and before we knew it chicken was banned from the house. Mom insisted, which isn't like her, but when it comes to Raff's well-being she seems to manage it. Dad and I even had to stop sneaking out for McNuggets on Saturdays because, three hours later, Raff could still "sense" it.

But enough of his good points. The first indication of Raff's absolute lack of morals burst in with a fanfare when he drowned one of my dolls in the bath. He couldn't have been more than five. After that her eyes never closed, as though she had to remain permanently awake in case he came for her again. Sometimes I'd widen my eyes like hers and try not to blink for as long as possible. Awful. To say that from that day forth Raff has embarked on a systematic destruction of my personal happiness, and that I have eyed him with mistrust ever since, would be totally accurate.

Perhaps the most teeth-grindingly annoying thing about him is that he never gets caught. His crimes seem to pass people by ("people" being Mom and Dad). They don't know he smokes cigarettes, they don't know that he's driven the car at least twice in the middle of the night (that I know of, and I've got better things to do than be on his case constantly, so it could be hundreds of times), and they *definitely* don't know that he's dabbled in prescription drugs. It's not as if I've never tried to bring it to their attention. But somehow I've never been able to make it sound true. I always end up looking like a liar. Motivation: just being a pain-in-the-butt big sister, Mom figures.

Someone knocks lightly on my bedroom door. It isn't Dad. He used to just barge in, until the day Mom and I went out shopping and came home with my first bra. Now he does a hefty *rap-ra-ra-rap-rap*-pause-*rap-rap* and waits for me to open it myself, and he always looks around the room before getting on with whatever he's come to say, as if he's worried about what frightening piece of teenage girl paraphernalia might jump out at him.

It isn't Raff. He doesn't have a knock, exactly, but a series of irritating noises: a dull whistle through the keyhole, or an unconvincing *coo*.

So, by process of elimination . . .

"Come in, Mom," I say.

She pokes her head around the door.

"How did you know it was me?"

I shrug and pop my iPod into the speaker, put on some background music.

Mom comes all the way in, closes the door, and stands just to the right of it, craning her neck. She looks more like she's come for a job interview than a mother-daughter pep talk.

"Did you want something?" I say, probably more curtly than I should have, judging by the injured look on her face.

"I just wondered how you were." She goes to sit on my unmade futon, lowering herself smoothly instead of flopping down like any normal person. "This is nice, what's this?" She means the music.

"Just a song I thought I'd practice for my audition." I stare at her until she realizes that I'm being sarcastic. Her mouth nervous-twitches into a weak smile, and she tries to pull her skirt over her knees but it won't go.

"I had no idea he was planning this," she says to the carpet.

"I know."

Dad announces things, he doesn't ask for opinions. There's never any warning about what mood he's going to be in, either, only we know that On The Up can last for weeks on end, but the GTDs usually don't last the month. Except for last time.

"You know what he's like," she says.

"Yep." This is us having a deep and meaningful.

"It's only because he's proud of you, Kass. He believes in you. We're not all so lucky as to have that kind of . . ." Her voice trails off. She has a habit of not finishing her sentences.

"I don't *feel* very lucky." There's a burning sensation in my throat telling me that I need to nip this conversation in the bud unless I want a grand-scale scene on my hands. Izzy and Char are always asking why I never try to get Mom on my side to help me fend off Dad when he's cooking up something horrifying to ruin my life. All they see is this beautiful, calm, rational, *nice* woman, and she is, but I can't rely on her for disasters like this. Dealing with Dad's GTDs saps all her energy, and there's nothing left for me.

At least I don't have to worry about her making things worse; I just wish I could rely on her to make things easier. I know she used to make me feel better—Band-Aids on skinned knees, bedtime stories, chicken soup (before the ban)—but I need something a bit stronger now.

"It's just that doing this for you makes him so . . . happy," she says, as if *happy* is a word like *cancer* that people like my mom find really awkward to get out. We stare at each other until she looks away, and now there is something so heavy between us it's as if the figure of Dad hunched over on the floor, lost in one of his darkest moods, is right between us.

44

I'm not stupid—I can see why Mom would want me to just get on with it instead of kicking up a fuss. Right now Dad's on Planet Up, which orbits yours truly and means that everyone else gets a holiday. For me, Dad's *happy* isn't exactly contagious. At least I hope not.

"Isn't it nice that he believes in you," she says, not quite a question but a statement. "Look, you don't want to end up like me."

"Why, what are you that I don't want to end up like?"

"Well, I'm a slave in that office, you know that. And *here* I'm . . . well, I'm your mother, and that's wonderful, but . . ."

But? I know she'd never finish the *but.*

"I don't see why it has to be a choice between slave and pop star," I say. "Slave or Oscar-nominated actress. Slave or Nobel Prize–winning scientist. Office Secretary or Secretary of State. Why is it always extremes? What about all the things in between?"

"I know, Kass. I just . . . look, we both know how difficult Christmas was, and I think this is a *good* sign, overall. We don't want to . . ."

It's as if her brain short-circuits the minute she's about to say something real.

"We don't want to *what?* Make him barricade us in again, or obsessively Google carbon-steel-armored doors with patented locking systems while he rapidly smokes himself to death? *What?*"

Mom turns her face as if I've just slapped her, and I grab

45

a discarded sweater and bury my face in it. It stinks of Dad's cigarettes.

"Kass! Let's not do this now. Don't upset yourself any more. Please." It looks like this meeting has been adjourned. She gets up with that same fluid motion, stoops to come nearer to me, and puts her hand on my shoulder. I flinch and feel guilty all at once, but I just can't let myself get upset in front of her, otherwise I'll start to want things from her that I know — while I'm still slightly rational — she won't be able to give me.

"OK, sweetheart," she says. She's *so* forgiving. "I'll leave you in peace."

She closes the door with the care of someone trying not to wake a baby.

Peace? She thinks she's leaving me in *peace?* As soon as she's gone I throw down the sweater and start to pull fistfuls of my hair until it feels like a layer of my scalp will peel away. I have to think, I have to plan, I have to get myself out of this. My scalp aches and I breathe deeply and sit cross-legged on the floor, head in hands.

It's not self-deprecation to say that I can't hold a tune; it's called having ears. My voice hovers somewhere between tone-deaf and almost bearable if I sing very quietly.

But this isn't as simple as lining up in the cold, singing half a bar, thanking the judges for their comments, and going home. This is My Whole Entire Life for the next few weeks — eating, sleeping, breathing, talking nonstop *X Factor*. This means no going out, no having friends over. This is Dad pouring every ounce of energy into something he believes in more than most people believe in gravity, which means there *is* actually a chance in hell that he might somehow, *somehow*, get me past the first round and into boot camp. It would have zero to do with me and everything to do with him if that happened, but he has his ways—he'll wear them down, if nothing else. He is a salesman and I am a bag of sour lemons! Just add sugar.

And whenever I fail, which I always do (without fail), we have to go through the whys, and I feel like a dead body in the morgue being picked apart. This is followed by a range of conspiracy theories that are less plausible than alien landings. And afterward, even though it signals the end and I should be thankful, there is that moment when he realizes that it's really over, and the look on his face . . . It is not a simple look; there are layers to it.

Then there's the next morning: the feeling of dread as I walk downstairs, searching Mom's face for a sign that he's OK, he hasn't slipped into another bad cycle. You just never know.

Izzy thinks Dad's easy to feel guilty about because he has lots of childlike qualities. She knows a lot of stuff like that because she's been in therapy for two years over her parents' divorce. But I hated it when she said it, as if she was looking down on Dad.

Not all of Dad's qualities are childlike, anyway; some of them are just plain weird. For example, Dad's favorite movie is *National Velvet*, which is about a little girl who pretends to be a boy so she can win a horse race. As if it's not bad enough that he can't like something normal and dadlike, he actually quotes lines from it when my friends are over: "Someday you'll learn that greatness is only the seizing of opportunity, clutching with your bare hands till the knuckles turn white." And he actually makes fists till the blood drains away, and holds them up for everyone to see. When you have a dad like that, you can tell who your real friends are by the people who show up a second time.

Even my name comes from his conviction that what we're called determines who we are or how successful we'll be. That's why he nipped Pidge in the bud. (*"My daughter, a common pigeon?"*) Kassidy means . . . wait for it . . . *clever*. Which is stupid. First, it's stupid, because the word *Kassidy* does not *sound* clever at all. Second, I'm not. I'm OK; I'm average. I know this because in a class of thirty students I'm fifteenth in every single subject on just about any occasion, except if someone is out sick, and it doesn't take a genius to do the math of how average that is; it takes someone of *average* intelligence. Me.

I might not be up to much in the IQ department, but there's got to be some way to ease myself out of this stupid audition. I've just got to go about it gently, back away without any sudden movements.

Rap-ra-ra-rap-rap-pause-*rap-rap*.

Speak of the devil.

"Yes, Dad, come in," I say, with all the enthusiasm of a cold, wet sponge.

"Everything all right?" he says.

"Actually, no, Dad, I'm not doing it."

OK, I seem to be going for the direct approach instead.

48

"Excuse me?"

"No."

"No?"

"I said no, I do not excuse you for interfering in my life *again*."

"Don't speak to me like that, I'm your father." Our voices rise in volume a little more with each sentence.

"So, then, as my father, why don't you respect what I want?"

"You don't know what you want, Kassidy."

"I do!"

"Oh, yes? Please tell me, then."

"Why should I?"

"Now you're being a baby. I know what's best for you. And it's not boys, before you start getting any ideas."

"I'm fifteen, Dad. You can't make me do things like this anymore."

"Come on, Kassidy, I'm not *making* you. I do all this *for* you, you've got to understand that." He starts to turn red in the face and shaky. "I never had parents who believed in me like I believe in you."

Shit. Why does he have to do this? It's like he's the only one who's allowed to feel *anything.*

"What, you mean they actually let you make your own decisions?" I say. He slams the door and I jump a little.

"*You* don't know what—" He stops. He's out of breath and his eyes are about as wide as they can get. He's right; I don't know what his parents were like. We've been here before—and when I say *here*, I mean this awkward pause just before Dad *might* tell

49

us something about his past, because as far as we know he came into existence sometime in his twenties, when he met Mom.

He takes a deep breath and gently opens the door, as if he can undo the slamming. When he next speaks he's calm again.

"I don't ever want you to feel like you're not good enough, Kassidy; to have someone wreck your dreams. I've made the most of what little I had, but for you there is so much more."

Inside, I am screaming at him: *But these aren't my dreams! These are* your *dreams! I don't want more; I don't want fame.* It is *too much* that it is up to me to wipe that tragic look off his face. But I know that this is not going to be the time that I get through to him. I'm not totally spineless—I've said no before; I regretted it. *Everyone* regretted it. There has to be another way out.

"Actually, Dad, I'm just getting dressed, so . . ."

"Yes, yes, of course. I'll go. Don't be mad at your old dad." He hunches up with his hands in a begging position and alarmingly reminds me of Gollum. Oh, this is precious, all right. I can't like him because he keeps messing up my life, but I can't hate him, either. And I shouldn't pity him, should I?

I'm fifteen, and I can't even stand up to my dad. One more fail.

✳ *Chapter Four* ✳

All I Want for Christmas Is a Carbon-Steel-Armored Door with Patented Locking System

For the rest of the day I'm locked in my room. When I say locked, I really mean that I've wedged a flip-flop under the door so that entry will be slow, if not impossible. Dad won't let us have real locks on our bedroom doors. Which is ironic.

Luckily I can survive on emergency rations:

* last night's by-the-bed water (complete with mysterious bubbles);
* the Rolo that Char taped onto a homemade Valentine's card last year . . . or possibly the year before;
* a pear from my schoolbag (except for the gross part imprinted by my spiral-bound notebook);
* an entire bag of tortilla chips that I bribed Raff to get for me by sending him a text to say that, yes, I had noticed that he'd recently eBayed three of Dad's DVD box sets.

In between snacking, I've been staring at the computer screen, hoping that the blank Word document will miraculously fill up with sentences that form an A+ essay entitled: *Discuss examples of ways in which Willy Loman's suicide is foreshadowed in the first act of the play*. Not that I ever got an A+ in my entire life, or possess the power of telekinesis. It would probably help if I read the play, or if I could ever bear to have the book faceup on my desk instead of hidden under a magazine and a packet of astringent wipes. *Death of a Salesman*—just a little too close to home what with my dad being (a) a salesman and (b) let's not go there. When the book first got handed out in class I skipped to the notes in the back, so I already know that it's about the *actual* death of an *actual* salesman, not just the death of his career, which I suppose would be quite a boring play and not exactly a "tragedy."

Eventually I stop pretending I can ever hope to concentrate on the essay and fully commit to buying one from Raff later (another secret and profitable sideline of his, which not even Izzy and Char know I take advantage of). I check my e-mail approximately once every thirty seconds until something comes through from a random person on Facebook who friended me weeks ago saying she was Char's cousin's friend from middle school.

Rachel Olsen has invited you to take the WHAT MENTAL DISORDER DO YOU HAVE? quiz. C'mon, we know you must have something!

I get a lurch in my diaphragm that very nearly gives the tortilla chips an encore, and delete the e-mail. I know it's random and she probably sent it to another fifty people, but it *feels* personal. Now I'm stuck with a bouncy voice inside saying: *We know you must have something!*

I don't. I don't have anything.

We know you must have something!

I'm normal. I'm as sane as you can get. I inherited his nose, nothing else. Except his feet. And hair. That's it. Oh, and his poor blood circulation, love of spicy food, and highly sensitive skin. But nothing else.

C'mon, now. Take the quiz!

No! I don't need a quiz. I'm perfectly healthy.

Really? Then what are all these voices in your head? We KNOW you must have something!

So I log in to Facebook. *Why should you take this quiz?* it says. *Because it's fun!* it says. Fine. I can do fun. I *know* it's just a stupid quiz that doesn't mean anything—in fact, I'm proving to myself how little it means by taking it. If I had anything to hide, I wouldn't be able to do that, right?

What if you don't like the answer you get? it says. *You can just take the quiz again!* it says. Perfect. Just like real life.

I answer all ten questions really quickly and think to myself that the multiple choice doesn't give you any chance to come out as "sane."

How would your friends describe you?

a. Obsessive?

b. Paranoid?

c. In a world of your own?

There is no *d. Very well-adjusted to reality and an all-around awesome friend.* Then I click *Find out your disorder!* and it asks me to select twenty of my friends to send the quiz to before I can see my results. No way. So I shut the whole thing down and switch off the monitor and turn up the music and flop onto my bed.

I feel ashamed for even thinking about doing the quiz. It's not fun, it's wrong. They wouldn't make a *What Cancer Are You?* quiz, would they? With a cutesy: *C'mon, we know you're gonna get it!* But somehow it's OK to make fun of mental illness. It's OK to forget that people suffer from it and that their friends and family suffer, too.

Now I'm fired up and on my feet. I log in again and click *Block This Application*, shut the computer down again, and start picking up clothes and putting away shoes and books, because the room feels small and cluttered all of a sudden.

When it's tidy I lie on the floor and listen to the pigeons. I'm calm again. It's nice just being quiet and alone; I bet I could stay up here for an entire week. I've got enough dirt on Raff to bribe him for more supplies. In fact, if I just barricade myself in here, maybe I could even survive until after the *X Factor* audition. I could probably pull the dresser down on its side if I emptied it first, and it could go right across the door, and then the shelves could go on top of that, and that cello is pretty heavy — might as well be used for something, since I can't get a note out of it that doesn't sound like a groaning zombie.

I turn onto my front — facing the door — to build up a

mental picture of the barricade: dresser, drawers, cello, filled suitcase — no, the cello should go on top of the filled suitcase . . . Dresser, drawers, filled suitcase, cello. Perfect!

Oh.

My blood literally runs cold — I thought that was just an expression, but it turns out it can actually happen when you're visited by the Ghost of Christmas Past. . . .

. . . It was December 17. I remember because before I went downstairs for breakfast I turned the date in my school planner into a stupid doodle of a stick figure of a girl holding a cocktail glass and wrote: *Xmas shopping with I & C!* in the A.M. section and *C's B-day Party! (buy new mascara)* in the P.M. section.

At the kitchen table, I didn't notice until afterward that Mom was quieter than usual, but that's because Mom's normal level is so quiet anyway that it's like telling the difference between a breeze and a breath. Raff had taken the last of the peanut butter, but I decided that was for the best because I wanted to look thin for the party. The three of us were eating toast, and I think I was talking about whether Char's megastrict dad would still make us play musical chairs at her party.

Then we all stopped.

Dad stood in the doorway. The famous Gray Tracksuit was saggy at the knees and almost the same color as his face. He held the butt of a cigarette and looked at Raff and me as if we were strangers.

"Cup of tea?" Mom said. He nodded and left, and then

there was the sound of the television coming on. Mom got up and kissed the top of my head and squeezed my shoulders, and I thought: Is that her way of telling me this GTD is not my fault? And if it even occurred to her to reassure me, doesn't that mean it really *is* my fault?

I looked at Raff to see if he thought so, too. But he got up and put on his jacket, said something about meeting a friend, and headed for the door.

"WAIT!" Dad boomed. Mom and I rushed into the living room. Dad was pointing the remote control at Raff, whose hand was frozen on the latch.

"What is it?" said Raff, trying to look cool, though I could see that the boom had gone straight through him like it had us.

"Nobody leaves." Dad turned the television up and flicked through the channels like he always did when he was in this mood—sometimes he'll let us watch almost an entire program and then change the channel before the last ten minutes.

"What do you mean, Paul?" said Mom. She handed him his tea. He drinks it nonstop when he's like that. Smokes nonstop, too. Eats nothing, except the odd yogurt or a bowl of cereal. Sleeps in the day.

"I mean what I say. Nobody leaves. Look, please don't make this difficult. I've had a terrible night and I just need to sit here and think a while." He scratched his right temple with the remote control and then put it down and lit another cigarette.

"But Dad, I'm supposed to be meeting Izzy and Char. We're doing our Christmas shopping," I said.

"Not today," he said. He didn't look at me, just flicked through the channels and chain-smoked and slurped tea.

Raff went upstairs in his jacket without saying a word. I knew he was going out his bedroom window, and I knew I couldn't do the same, and that made me angrier than ever.

"Mom, it's Char's party tonight. You have to do something."

She ushered me past Dad and up the stairs, whispering, "*Sshh*, it's OK. Don't upset yourself now. Just go upstairs and keep out of his way for today and we'll work something out."

"What do you mean?" I whispered back.

"*Sshh*, trust me. I'll be up in a minute."

I can remember feeling a tiny bit excited by the look on her face and by the fact that she wasn't just admitting defeat. I felt proud of her, and tingly inside because maybe it would be me and Mom fighting the GTD together, not letting it get the better of us.

She came into my bedroom about half an hour later.

"He's OK. He's taking a nap," she said.

"What's going on? Why doesn't he want us to go out?"

"He was up all night watching the news. Some poor man was stabbed on his doorstep. A family man — he'd only gone out to ask a group of boys to turn their music down. Tragic."

I didn't say anything for a while. Mom was staring at the floor as if she was still thinking about it, and I didn't want to interrupt or seem callous. Then she snapped out of it and gave my room a look that made me feel bad for being such a slob, which seemed a bit irrelevant at a time like this.

"Well, yes, that *is* tragic. But how does it affect me going shopping?" I said.

"It won't be forever. You know how sensitive he is. He just wants to protect us all and sometimes it weighs very heavily on him. Be a bit understanding, Kass."

"What, understanding about being a prisoner? We don't even live in a bad neighborhood. It's stupid—we can't live like that, we'd never go out. And what about the party? I'm not missing that."

"It's fine. I'll take you to the party. Leave it to me. Just—just try not to upset your dad today." As Mom left she was still giving my room the *Clean It* look, but my mind was juggling two completely separate thoughts:

1. *Is my dad right? Should we all be scared? Is the world a terrifying place?*
2. *I'm going to the party.*

For the rest of the day, Mom and I tiptoed around Dad. We told him Raff was upstairs playing Wii. Izzy and Char didn't question my texts about having to visit relatives instead of going shopping with them, and I knew I could make up whatever I liked later as long as I said it was Dad's side of the family, because we didn't know anything about them anyway so it seemed like one healthy step away from lying, somehow. More like "imagining."

I spent hours in the bathroom, planning my outfit and wondering if I should take the miniature bottles of Baileys I knew were stashed in the laundry room (Dad was supposed to be selling them as stocking stuffers for Christmas).

I was almost ready when Mom knocked on my door. As I opened it she held her finger to her lips and motioned for me to follow. We crept down the stairs, past their bedroom door, which was ajar and revealed a duvet-covered lump: Dad. While Mom got the car keys, I grabbed three miniature bottles and stuffed them in my pocket. We went out the back.

The rush was amazing as we clicked our seat belts and set off for Char's. My calf muscles were twitching and my heart was racing and I flipped down the sun visor to check my lipstick in the mirror, flipped it up again, smiling at Mom and trying really hard not to think about Dad waking up and finding us gone.

I don't remember much about the party, except that we didn't drink the Baileys. I know that Mom stayed downstairs in the kitchen being bored to death by Char's ultradull dad, while fifteen girls and Char's two boy cousins (ages twelve and fourteen, the only Y chromosomes allowed past the threshold) crammed into her room. The rest is a blur—I think I have a bizarre form of amnesia where I forget all the fun times and remember the traumatic ones.

When Mom tried the back door on our return, it was locked. She kept pressing down the handle and pushing the door, over and over, gently, but getting more anxious each time. We stood there for a while: me looking at her, her looking at the door handle.

"Maybe Raff locked it," she said. At that moment her phone beeped with a text message, and suddenly she started knocking loudly on the glass door.

"PAUL! PAUL!"

"Mom, what is it?" I said. Her face was taut, and she kept knocking and calling out for Dad to open up.

"You run around front and ring the bell," she said. But as I was leaving the back door opened.

"Quickly, quick, quick!" said Dad, with his arm stretched out to herd us in and sweat dripping from his brow as he scoured the backyard path over our heads.

Inside, the house was unrecognizable. Raff was on the stairs, half-concealed in shadow. The living room was empty except for Dad's armchair and the television, which was on the floor. Every piece of furniture — sofa, coffee table, bookcase, television cabinet, coatrack, kitchen table, chairs — was piled up by the front door.

Dad was out of breath, and came to stand between us and the barricade. He'd lit a cigarette.

"We've got to get this door changed," he said. "This door is not safe."

"Paul, what have you . . . ? OK, let's just calm down for a second," said Mom, pacing the empty space where our furniture had been.

"Me calm down?" said Dad. "You sneak out of the house with our young daughter and take her God knows where and I'm supposed to calm down?" He grabbed Mom by the shoulders. *"Anything could have happened!"*

She turned her face from him and I rushed over.

"Stop it, Dad, you're scaring me."

He looked at me as if he'd only just noticed I was in the room, and let Mom go. His face changed, seemed to soften from anger but then crumple into worry.

"Are you OK?" he said.

"What have you done, Dad?"

"It's OK, it's all right," said Mom, and she urged me over to the staircase. "I'll deal with this. Go to bed, you two." Raff had already disappeared.

"No, I want to stay," I said, but I felt such a lump in my throat that I knew I didn't want to at all—most of me wanted to run and hide, but it was like passing by an accident on the highway and your brain telling you not to look but your body unable to turn away.

"Let her stay," said Dad. His face changed again; the worry smoothed off. "I haven't seen her all day. Come on, the three of us. I'll make some coffee."

He went into the kitchen.

"What's happening?" I whispered.

"Um . . . he's just a bit upset. Don't worry."

"*Don't worry?* Look at this place."

She was; she was looking and nodding, but she wasn't giving anything away. Then Dad came back in clutching mugs of coffee—two in one hand, one in the other—concentrating hard because they were full to the brim. We were still over by the stairs. He handed the single mug to Mom, then handed one of the others to me. He took a sip of his and smiled at me.

"Cheers," he said. I said it back, with the barricade in the corner of my eye. I will never forget the look on his face when he turned back to face the room.

"Grace?" he said. His mug was shaking; Mom took it from him. "Grace, what happened?" He ran over to the barricade as if he'd never seen it before. Then he knelt in front of it, and his head fell to his chest and his body started to shake. He was crying.

Mom motioned for me to go upstairs, and I did, to the sound of my dad sniveling in front of his crazy paranoid barricade.

That night I shut it all out. I lay in the dark, in a ball, pressing the heels of my hands into my eye sockets until I saw colored spots and patterns, over and over until I finally fell asleep. The next day, the living room was back to normal. Dad was in the armchair, smoking. He had a piece of paper by his side, and I looked over his shoulder as I passed by on my way to the kitchen: *Carbon-Steel-Armored Door with Patented Locking System.*

I decide to give my bedroom a complete makeover, and play my music loud to drown out my thoughts. It's all OK, really: Tomorrow is Monday, so I get to blow all this buildup of family stuff out of my head and talk about ordinary things again. Plus Christmas is over—it was weeks ago—and we still have a perfectly normal front door.

✳ *Chapter Five* ✳

How to Poke a Finger in Your Best Friend's Bubble

We have a Monday morning routine on the 86. Traditionally, it has three stages — but only for me because I'm the first to get on the bus.

Stage 1: Kass's Virtually Aimless Brain Zigzag:

This morning I'm thinking about how I always get stuck with a part I *didn't* audition for, like when I had to be the donkey in a play in elementary school, or how I got the role of The Apple of His Eye in Dad's cringe-worthy show aka My Life, or why I'm the one out of me, Izzy, and Char who cracks the silly jokes that I seem to find funnier than they ever do.

Time's up! Izzy's stop.

Stage 2: Izzy's Latest Therapy-Based Observation:

"I've realized something," she says. I'd be more shocked if she *hadn't* realized something, because she's been theorizing since the days when we still wore undershirts. (Wow, remember undershirts? Simpler days.) Izzy sits sideways on the seat in front and puts her bag next to her. "OK, here it is: Opposites *attract*, but they don't *last*."

"Right."

"It's true. You see, my dad was attracted to the way my mom is really open about emotions and stuff, and my mom was attracted to the way my dad doesn't spill his emotions all over the place, as in, he let her concentrate on her own. But in the end, he drowned in hers and she sort of died of thirst waiting for his. See?"

"Makes sense, Izz." It's always best to agree. Izzy sits back, satisfied, as if she's just found the chemical formula for instant acne remover. And something occurs to *me* for a change. "So, you're saying that *ideally* we need someone who is the same as us." I'm trying not to smirk as I think about the Other Cass — OK, it's only the same name, but then how much of a sign can it be to get butterflies over someone with the same name? It's got to mean *something*.

"Not exactly the same. It's complicated." It always is with Izz. "Anyway, how are you feeling?" She has that phrase down pat now. The way she says it makes you instantly remember the horrible thing you were trying your best to forget. That's the Therapist Factor.

"Kind of . . . dunno."

"*Mmm.*" That *Mmm* is straight out of a psychotherapy text-book, too. It means: *Please continue.*

"My dad is really into it. It's like someone replaced him with a puppy who just discovered the toilet paper roll."

"*Mmm.* Can't you just be sick on the day?"

"I'd have to be in a coma. Anyway, the whole buildup to it is almost equally torturous. It's a lost cause."

"It can't be. You've just got to make your dad realize that he can't live out his dreams through you; it's not fair."

"I know, Dr. Freud"—Izzy love-hates when I call her that—"but just how do I do that?"

"You just have to stay calm and explain your feelings."

"Don't you think I've tried that?" I say, already not very calm, thanks. "You don't know my dad."

"But, Kass, you're fifteen. He can't *make* you."

I almost wish I hadn't told her now. She'll start waving self-help pamphlets at me any moment now.

Stage 3: Char's Latest Two-Second Conversation with the Boy of Her Dreams:

For nearly four years, Char has had a crush on an older boy who lives next door. This is about the only information we have on him, because Char is so superstitious she thinks that telling us any of his stats will jinx their "relationship." The crush might well have bordered on stalking were it not for the fact that she has the strictest dad in the world, who grounds her at every opportunity. *Bad grades? You're grounded, Charlotte. Home late? Grounded. Talking back? Grounded. Single strand of hair out of place? Grounded!!*

Dream Boy does sound dreamy, in a very vague sort of way, but since Char is so nice about everyone it's really hard to tell. Izzy always says that I'm so intolerant it makes it even more special when I really like someone. Isn't that what they call a backhanded compliment?

Char sits one seat in front of Izzy, sideways like her. She is obviously bursting to tell us something.

"Guess what?"

"He proposed," I say.

"He's gay," says Izzy.

"No, and no," says Char. She's much too levelheaded to rise to the usual bait, but that's another tradition.

"OK, we give up, tell us what happened," I say.

"OK!" Char is already at the clapping-squealing-seal stage and she hasn't even begun — this may indicate a conversation consisting of more than "Hi" after only four years! Gotta love the girl. At least she's out of that weird mood she was in last week.

"So I just happened to be coming out of my house as he was walking by with his brother, and he said 'Hi,' and I said 'Hi,' and then he stopped right in front of my gate and said, 'Hey, you go to St. Agatha's, don't you?' and I said, 'Yeah, why?' and he said, 'Nothing, just wondering. Anyway, see you.'"

She's smiling so broadly it looks as if her jawbone might split. I fear for her health if he ever actually asks her out.

"Why did he want to know, do you think?" says Izzy.

"I don't know!" squeals Char. It's clear that a million possibilities have already passed through her mind, not all of them rational.

"I guess he just wanted something more to say than 'Hi,'" I say. "There was this boy at my house yesterday who—"

"Oh-oh-oh, wait, that's not all," says Char. "His brother gave me this *really* weird look as they were going inside. Kind of pervy but strange. And I was, like, 'Yeah, right, Lucas, *as if*, you're thirteen, not gonna happen.' And it's, like, why won't his brother look at me like that?"

"Hey, that's weird," I say. "Raff has a friend like that. Actually, *his* name is Lucas."

They both smile at me for this irrelevant detail. Very polite, my friends.

"So what's the next step with Dream Boy?" says Izzy.

"Ooh, I don't know. Do you think he notices that I'm always coming out of my house when he's going into his?"

"Nah, he's a boy, they're thick," I say.

"*He's* not, he goes to Dudley, and that's really hard to get into." Char looks at me as if I've just stolen her lunch money.

"I didn't mean *he* was thick, Char," I say. "I just mean I doubt he's noticed because I'm sure you're very subtle, that's all."

The relief puts color in her cheeks again just as it's draining out of mine.

"Hang on, Char, did you say Dudley?"

"Yeah, why?"

I don't know why I didn't think of it before, or why I'm staring the obvious in the face and having such trouble spitting it out. It's no big deal.

"Char, his name isn't Cass, is it?"

"Yes, so? How do *you* know?"

"I don't believe it."

"*What?*"

"It can't be."

"*What* can't it be?"

Izzy sits more upright, possibly to get away from Char, who appears to be about to climb over the seat and shake it out of me.

"Umm, he was at my house yesterday, Char." It shouldn't be such a big deal. But I have this awful feeling it's going to be.

"Oh, please. Shut up."

"No, seriously. So you shut up."

"Come on, you two, no arguing," says Izzy. "What do you mean, Kass?"

Char has such a strange look on her face that I feel like saying I made it all up and just dealing with her thinking of me as a liar, which has to better than whatever she's thinking now. But my eyelid has started to twitch the way it does when I feel really guilty about something. I'll have to tell her.

"OK. Yesterday, Raff had a friend over. Pervy Lucas. Pervy Lucas has a big brother and he came to pick him up. He said his name was Cass and that he went to Dudley and he asked me if I went to St. Agatha's and I said I did and he seemed really nice and my dad made a total ass of himself in front of him and of course brought me down with him and so I had to escape upstairs and he probably thinks I'm really rude or something." It's a long sentence for one breath, but I had to let it all out quickly.

They are both completely silent.

"You've turned totally red," says Izzy quietly.

"No, I haven't."

"Yeah, you have," says Char, not quietly, and not like Char. Suddenly I feel ultradefensive.

"It's not *my* fault if he came to my house."

Char shrugs. Her eyes look shiny.

"Anyway, Char, he asked you what school you go to. That means he's interested in you, he wants to know things about you. That's a sign." I know I sound as unsure as she looks.

"He asked you, too, you said."

"That doesn't mean *anything*," I say. "You should have seen how tragic I was looking. I wasn't even dressed. Sweats and mascara smudges from the night before and major bedhead."

Char turns around in her seat and puts her bag on her lap. This has never happened before. I reach forward and tug the shoulder of her blazer.

"Hey, Char, don't be like that."

"Yeah, come on, Char," says Izzy. "Let's talk about this."

"Char, you're being ridiculous."

"Char, please."

"Char, I haven't even *done* anything."

But by now we can tell that she's crying. Half of me thinks: ARE YOU KIDDING ME? But the other half has that sinking feeling you get when you feel the crunch of a ladybug beneath your shoe. Izzy and I shrug at each other, and she mouths: *There must be more to it*, which I get after the third try. If there is, it's still with her now as she gets up without looking at us and goes to another empty seat near the exit way before we've reached our stop.

✳

I'm not the type to stop eating in a crisis. Stress makes me more hungry. Still, these cafeteria fries are agony to get down. Every one sticks in my throat, and I wonder why I couldn't have been more elegant and restrained and opted for healthy tuna salad like Izzy. That would be why *she's* willowy, I suppose. That and genes.

St. Agatha's fries are hardly worth having, anyway. They're not crisp and hot and greasy like fast-food fries, and served on cold plastic plates they taste like fries with their very souls sucked out. Then again, how comforting is limp lettuce? And I *do* feel like being comforted. Char has barely spoken to me since the bus ride. She chose the spaghetti with tomato sauce; I'm trying to decide what that means.

Every so often I catch Izzy and Char giving each other gentle smiles. I know Izzy's smile is designed to comfort Char rather than alienate me, but it dents my confidence every time I see it pass between them. This isn't the first time the Three of Us has become Two Plus One, but I think it's the first time I've felt like the One. I guess it had to be my turn sooner or later, but this doesn't feel like a good enough reason. She's being totally irrational—so why do I feel so guilty?

"French fry?" I say to Char.

"I've got spaghetti."

"I know. Just thought you'd like one."

"No, thanks."

"OK."

I know not to offer one to Izzy. She'd wrinkle her nose and

70

look at me as if I was voluntarily ingesting dog poo, and this lunch is unappetizing enough already.

"Anyone want another water?" I say. St. Agatha's girls can't be trusted with water pitchers on the tables. Instead we are given thimble-size plastic cups and have to trek to the back of the room to fill them up. We're only supposed to take two cups to fill at a time. It's touching how much they trust us to perform orangutan-level tasks.

Izzy raises her empty cup and nods with a mouthful of tuna. Char doesn't even look up.

"Char? What about you?"

"You've got Izzy's. You can only take two." She starts stabbing a meatball—unnecessarily hard, it seems to me.

"I can take Izzy's and yours. I don't mind."

"I'll get my own. Wouldn't want to deprive you."

"Char, I'm just trying to offer you a drink, would you just chill?"

She stops stabbing the meatball and her eyes fill up again. I slump back down in my seat.

"Char, *please*, what is it?" She snatches her arm away from my grip. This is insane. Izzy flicks her head toward the water cooler, so I take my cup and hers and leave.

While I'm filling them I can see Char wipe her eyes and nod and smile at Izz. Then they both get up and make their way to the exit. Izzy turns back and gives me a cute wave and a thumbs-up as they disappear to the coatroom, where secret conversations tend to take place among the heavy navy blue coats.

I down both drinks and head for the library, where people with no one else to hang out with at lunchtime tend to go.

I get to the art room first and start to prepare our table. Monday afternoons are always fun because the three of us get to sit together instead of in Two Plus One formation like all the other classes. We sit around tables facing each other as if we're in a café instead of in forward-facing rows of double desks like we do in every other subject. It's so much more civilized (i.e., nothing like school).

As I'm choosing the best brushes and paints, sharpening pencils with the knife the way we've been shown, and hitching up the desktop easels, I feel like I'm making up for something awful I've done. I couldn't have known that the Other Cass was Dream Boy, could I? I try to think back . . . I *couldn't* have known. And anyway, our meeting was a total disaster thanks to my fidgeting, my morning-after makeup, and my dad's ability to thwart the rare potential romance that comes my way. Not that someone like the Other Cass would ever be interested in me, so it's not really fair to blame Dad (but it helps).

Char doesn't usually do drama. She's the leveler, the voice of reason; she's the kind of nice that makes you feel permanently sinful, but in a way that makes you want to hang out with her anyway. I feel pretty mature that I'm trying so hard to be sweet to Char even though she's the one who's being unreasonable. I guess she must really, really like him. That coatroom therapy session with Izzy better have fixed this — Char has always been more open to Izzy's talks than me.

Ms. Wallace has already started the class when Izzy and Char arrive, arm in arm. Izzy looks taller, and Char's eyes are red-rimmed.

"Sorry, Ms. Wallace, we had to stop at the nurse."

"Fine. Take a seat." Ms. Wallace is one of the more human(e) teachers at St. Agatha's. Maybe it's the Art Factor—she dresses in flouncy boho clothes and has cropped hair dyed peroxide blond, and you can tell she used to wear a nose ring—because it's not as if Art is about getting things wrong or right. In my experience, you either suck at it or you don't, and no amount of strictness is going to change that. She seems to have realized this, too. I'm on the right side of not sucking. Just.

"OK, everyone, today we're sketching portraits of each other, but I want you to follow the principles of the Surrealist movement that we discussed last week." She means putting an ear where the nose should be. No problem: I'm already feeling chaotic.

"There are reference books here at the front if anyone needs a refresher. You can talk as long as the levels don't start to interrupt my magazine reading." She's kidding. "I'm kidding. I'll be around to discuss your work with you. OK, get started."

The room slowly rouses itself with the scraping of chairs and hushed convos about who's going to draw whom. It's easy for most because the culture at St. Agatha's is a bit like Noah's Ark. Izzy and Char and I have always prided ourselves on being able to exist as a successful trio with none of the usual bitching or three's-a-crowd syndrome. *Syndrome!* Sounds like an Izzy word. I guess it's inevitable that our little ways rub off on each other, though I don't seem to have inherited her willowyness or Char's (usually) half-full instead of half-empty view of the world. Bummer.

"So, how should we do this?" I say. I've decided to go for the Let's Forget Our Troubles and Have Fun approach, and hope I'm not overdoing it with the full-frontal grin and cheery voice.

"It's up to you," Char says with a shrug. She doodles a spiral in the corner of her pad.

"No, c'mon—it's up to all of us!" I say, struggling to keep up the cheer. She shrugs again. "Izz, who do you want to draw?"

"I think the fairest way is if I draw Char, Char draws you, and you draw me."

I wonder if my efforts to figure out if that really *is* a fair way are noticeable on my face—sometimes things that come easily to some people take me a while to get. (You see now why Mensa might not have been beating my door down?) Izzy's the best at art, so at least if she draws Char, Char will get to see a cool picture at the end—and who doesn't like to see a cool picture of themselves? I only hope that Izzy's art skills can somehow get past the weirdness of Surrealism so that Char comes out looking pretty even if she has wonky eyes and a skyscraper coming out of her forehead. Or whatever. (Maybe I should check out those reference books before I start.)

"Sounds good," I say. "Char?"

Shrug

That girl's going to get repetitive stress injury if she shrugs any more. My patience is rapidly eroding—must . . . fight . . . it! Must . . . stay . . . NICE!

"Let's do that, then," says Izzy. She rubs Char's arm as if she's worried our newly quiet friend might be cold. I just know it would be a bad idea for me to do the same.

For the first time ever, we draw in silence. We might as well be in Math. Smiles don't make it full circle: Izzy smiles while she's drawing Char; Char's face is like stone when she looks at me, though she giggles self-consciously when Izzy is really staring at her; I stop trying to smile at Char and instead smile at Izzy, but my eyebrows are trying to form questions, like *What the hell is going on? What did Char say to you in the Secret World of Heavy Blue Coats? Why do I feel like the worst person on earth when all I did was answer my front door to a boy in brown boots?* All that just with eyebrows; I know Izzy understands every twitch, but all her eyebrows are saying back to me is *Be patient.*

Ms. Wallace is making her rounds. We're next. I should be able to tell by her facial expression whether Char has drawn me as a Snaggle-Toothed Acne-Covered Wildebeest. She stands behind Izzy first.

"That's very touching, Isobel, you've captured the melancholy in Charlotte; good job. I like your lines. Very self-assured. Try to go just a little harder around the eyes; I think you'll like the effect. Nice work."

Great, so Izzy is capturing some sadness in Char that I apparently put there! Now we'll have a permanent reminder of it. Ms. Wallace stands behind Char.

"This is interesting," she says, checking out Char's portrait of me. Interesting, or hideous? I need more to go on than that, Ms. Wallace. There's a Best Friend Crisis playing itself out here! Ms. Wallace looks at me, and then at the portrait. Me. Portrait. Me. Portrait. *What is it, Ms. Wallace?*

Then I catch Izzy bending slightly to see what Char has drawn.

"Keep at it," Ms. Wallace says to Char, with a squeeze of her shoulder. I shiver at the thought of mass conspiracy.

"Can I see?" I say. Without looking up, Char says:

"Nope. Not finished."

"I don't mind."

Char shakes her head and sniffs, takes a used tissue out of her sleeve, and dabs her eyes. She's like a faucet today! Fine, I don't want to see it, anyway; she's probably given me two heads.

Now Ms. Wallace is behind me.

"What pencil are you using?" she says.

"Umm . . . 2H?"

"It's wishy-washy, Kass. Try something darker and softer. You're not getting any depth. Maybe have another look at the books on my desk for inspiration, OK?"

Ms. Wallace leaves the ten-inch knife sticking out of my back as she continues her tour of the room. Izzy gives me a look I interpret as *Poor you, but you should have used the darker pencil, you know.* I look at my portrait, which apparently has no depth and no inspiration. She's right. And I have just slipped over onto the wrong side of sucking. I'm a Snaggle-Toothed Acne-Covered Wildebeest who can't draw and makes her friends miserable. And it's only Monday.

✳ *Chapter Six* ✳

The Curious Incident of the Mystery IMer

I can tell what kind of day Mom's had by what she makes us for dinner. Tonight it's spaghetti with stir-in carbonara sauce, as in the kind you don't even have to heat up (but should, because otherwise the spaghetti is cold in seconds flat, and who wants to eat tepid spaghetti in a congealed cream sauce?). This dish spells stress.

Right at the top of the Good Day scale we have the Roast. A roast dinner on a weeknight means that Mom's boss spent the day in meetings away from the office rather than annoying her. (She's a personal assistant to a man who Dad says must have grown up with the kind of fussing full-time nanny who was still wiping the corners of his mouth when he was in his teens. Now that's Mom's job.)

Further down we have Grilled Salmon with Fingerling Potatoes and Sugar Snap Peas, which means he only asked her to do five impossible things, four of which she was able to complete (the fifth was probably "Get me a double-thick unicorn milk shake from the planet Jupiter").

One up from the bottom of the heap is this Slightly Insipid Spaghetti Carbonara, which means he ran Mom ragged from 8:30 A.M. till 7 P.M. and then gave her a list of impossible things to be finished by tomorrow, just as he was leaving to enjoy a five-star meal somewhere swanky with the latest bimbette he's picked up. He's creepy-ancient, and Dad says he dates girls who are only a few years older than me.

But at least he hasn't fired Mom again. About once a month Mom gets fired for anything from looking at him the wrong way to wearing a scarf he finds annoying to putting too much milk in his coffee—and that means Weeknight Takeout. Raff and I try not to revel in this monthly occasion, but since Mom always gets her job back the next day it seems wrong not to enjoy a nice beef and broccoli with egg rolls and fortune cookies.

"Got a lot of work to do tonight, Mom?" I say. She's been fiddling with her hair and jolts suddenly when she realizes I'm talking to her.

"Umm, what? Oh, yes, a ton." Must have been a hard day—she's all jittery and keeps clearing her throat, and that must be her high heel I can hear tapping, because Dad is in his study smoking his brains out (though not in his tracksuit) and Raff is wearing those stupid giant Rudolph the Red-Nosed Reindeer slippers Mom bought him for Christmas last year. His BlackBerry is on the table, and he's typing while he swizzles spaghetti around his fork, and he almost makes his mouth every time. And I thought boys couldn't multitask.

"Actually, I'll probably have to go back out for a bit," says Mom.

"Why, what does he want you to do now?"

"Ugh, don't ask." She looks really on edge.

Damn, that means I'll be alone and defenseless. I had a nanochance of getting out of whatever Dad's cooking up for me in the study by persuading Mom to have a girly night of pampering—she'd straighten my hair, I'd paint her toes—because Dad avoids girly things like the plague. (He probably thinks we talk about boobs and periods, which is ridiculous because Mom is the kind of Lady who doesn't really get into conversations like that, as opposed to Izzy's mom, who wants you to tell her *evvverythiiing*.)

Raff leaves the room without a word. He's probably busy transferring funds to his offshore account, and anyway no one would believe me if I said I wanted to spend the evening doing something with him of all people.

Mom gets up and scrapes almost an entire plate of spaghetti into the garbage. If I was that stressed I'd have eaten double, followed by cake, followed by more cake, with ice cream. Sometimes I wonder if Mom and I are really related. Maybe they gave her the wrong baby in the hospital. Except I do have Dad's irritatingly curly hair, and although Dad manages to take over almost everything in this house, I really doubt he was the one who did the giving-birth part. He hollers if he gets a paper cut.

When the doorbell rings, Mom drops her plate.

"Oh! The door!" she says. She freezes and just stares at the door in terror, as if she's been on the run from the law and the jig is finally up. Like my mom could even steal a free mint from a restaurant.

"Chill out, Mom, I'll get it."

I open the door to approximately fifty red roses (I know they come in multiples of twelve, but this is no time for math) and a small voice behind them saying:

"For the lady of the house."

For the first time in my life I want to be The Lady. *"Let me be The Lady!"* I want to scream. *I'm The Lady! Me! Right here! All ladylike!* Almost all of my body tries not to want the card to be signed *The Other Cass.* Kiss kiss. Et cetera.

"Mom, they're for you," I say, with all the joy of a girl who's never even been kissed, except for once in a game of Seven Minutes in Heaven with creepy David who always had a cold sore. And one time with Izzy when we were ten. "They're from . . . Mr. Sizzle. Um, who the hell's he?"

"Me, of course! Who else?" In bounds Dad, like a spring lamb who's been mainlining Red Bull. He grabs Mom and kisses her as she makes these really strange yelping noises, which sound more like crying than happiness. This whole scene is doing nothing for the Parents Are Not So Weird campaign.

Mom puts the roses in vases until the vases run out and she has to use the coffeepot, a spaghetti sauce jar, and a rinsed-out orange juice carton. She just keeps saying, "I can't believe you did this." Dad is singing some old song they used to dance to, apparently. Now I know where I get my unique talent from.

Poor Dad looks a bit forlorn as Mom gathers her things and heads out the door, practically doubled over apologizing for having to work tonight. How can she leave when he's been so romantic? I don't know, but I'm thinking maybe one rose would have been enough. That's just not how my dad does things, though.

So then it's just him and me, and my least favorite word of the moment:

Rehearsal.

I could not hate the sound of my own voice more. My first attempt to put Dad off the whole *X Factor* idea has failed miserably — clearly he is only too willing to listen to out-of-tune performances of songs he hates for hours on end. The proud look on his face seems oddly unconnected to the sound that comes out of my mouth. He's some kind of aural masochist. Wow, that *is* a big word for me.

I must speak to someone normal before I go to sleep; I dial from my bedroom refuge. The decision of who to call is pretty easy based on today's activities, but it beeps to voice mail.

"You've reached Dr. Barbara Franklin and Isobel Franklin. Please leave us a brief message and we'll get back to you. Take care!"

The instruction to be brief always makes me panic.

"Hi, Izz, it's me. . . . Ummm, nothing important, just felt like talking. OK, so maybe I'll speak to you later, OK, hope you're well, and hi, Mrs. Franklin, if that's you listening, I mean Dr. Franklin—I mean Barbara. OK, sorry for the long message, bye!"

I've surpassed myself.

After only five minutes in here the tip of my nose feels like ice—my radiator's been broken for a couple of weeks, but if I tell Dad he'll get his tool kit out and that's not something I like to encourage. Before I know it, he'll have caused some unnatural disaster that will mean I have to vacate the room for an inde-terminable length of time, which will mean I have to share my personal space and oxygen supply with Raff, which would be . . . *shudder*

I switch on my computer. Maybe it was Izzy's mom hogging the phone and I'll be able to IM Izzy instead. It'd be helpful if Char was on, too, because I come across much better online than in person and I might even be able to snap her out of her mood. But Char's dad has blocked just about every worthwhile computer program and website. He's like some kind of über censor, and he's been worse since Char's mom left them. Even a fifteen-year-old can tell that the way he behaves is more likely to drive people away than protect them. It's basic common sense. He's lucky that Char is so understanding . . . most of the time.

Izzy's online.

tallgirl: hi, on phone, how u?
curlygirl: who on phone to?
tallgirl: char

curlygirl: how she?

tallgirl: ok sort of

curlygirl: whats going on? dont you think shes overreacting?

tallgirl: she very sensitive

curlygirl: yeah i know shes my friend 2

tallgirl: i didnt say she wasnt

curlygirl: i know

It's hard to tell with IMs, but I have a feeling Izzy's being frosty with me. What's the matter with me today? I'm hemorrhaging friends. Fortunately, I know what makes Izzy tick.

curlygirl: what do u think i should do izz?

tallgirl: u should say sorry and promise u wont do anything with db

curlygirl: WHAT??? say sorry for what? havent done anything!

tallgirl: well u asked. and don't shout

curlygirl: what would i say sorry for tell me!!

tallgirl: shes convinced ur going to steal db from her. u sounded like u'd fallen 4 him just from 1 meeting

curlygirl: i did??

tallgirl: yup u turned red were talking v fast was v obvious kass

curlygirl: nw thats so stupid db is hers!!! as if id do that

tallgirl: i know that but chars upset. wait . . . have to go char hears typing

curlygirl: fine bye

tallgirl: dont b mad. see u on bus. dont worry we will work it out

* tallgirl has gone offline. *

I feel like my best friend just slammed the door in my face. It's eerie how far the computer can suck you in, and how quickly it can spit you out again. I scan the rest of my contact list but there's no one I feel like talking to. I'm just about to quit when:

* stix wants to chat. Allow stix? *

Do I know a stix? I try to think what the screen name could mean. Stix . . . sticks . . . stick figure . . . someone with skinny legs? Almost everyone in my class has skinny legs, except me, who has just-a-bit-bigger-than-normal ones, and Michelle, who doesn't have skinny anything. It could be a total stranger— I'm not sure I'm in the mood for new web friends, though considering I'm doing so badly with my actual friends, what the hell?

* Allow stix. *
stix: Is this working?
curlygirl: is what working?
stix: Oh hi. It is working then. I've never used this before.
curlygirl: not 2 b rude but who are u?
stix: Guess.
curlygirl: not in mood sorry

stix: Why, what's up?

curlygirl: might tell u if u tell me who u are

stix: Just guess.

curlygirl: give me clue

stix: Ask me a question.

curlygirl: this is tedious. OK do u have skinny legs?

stix: Hope not, why?

(For the first time I contemplate that stix might be a boy. I don't know any girls who don't want skinny legs. It says a lot that I just assumed it'd be a girl—boys are few and far between in my humble existence, thanks to an all-girls' school, a younger brother, and not really having the sort of hair, face, or body that makes boys buzz around me bee-to-honey style the way they do around some of the girls in my class. Izzy and Char and I are all pretty much even when it comes to experience. We don't have any.)

curlygirl: what does stix stand for then?

stix: Drumsticks

curlygirl: i dont know any drummers

stix: Except for me.

curlygirl: grrr why dont u just tell me who u r?

stix: This is more fun.

curlygirl: for u maybe

stix: So far, so good. Ask more questions.

curlygirl: maybe I have better things to do

stix: Probably. Like practice for your audition?

My heart stops. This exchange has dramatically lowered the number of people stix could be. Who knows about my audition? Mom, Raff (and therefore Raff's idiotic bunch of followers, but there's no way any of them could maintain this kind of conversation and keep my interest, so they're out), Izzy, and therefore Izzy's therapist, and Izzy's mom, maybe Char, and therefore maybe Char's dad since he listens in on all her phone calls. And *my* dad, of course. He was in a band in the seventies. *Please* tell me stix isn't . . .

curlygirl: dad????
stix: I really doubt it. I was only three when you were born. Are you some kind of sicko? ☺

(Three plus fifteen equals eighteen. Wait, let me check: yes, definitely eighteen. But I don't know anyone who's eighteen, except for my cousin Jodie, but she lives in Ohio and her mom doesn't speak to my mom. I am developing a very intense headache.)

stix: I have to say I'm hurt.
curlygirl: why, did u poke urself in the eye with ur drumsticks?
stix: Ha-ha. Lucas said you had a good sense of humor.

Bomb. Drops.
Light. On.

curlygirl: Cassian?
stix: Finally.

I have to get up from my desk and move away from the screen, as if he might be able to see my reaction. I fall awkwardly onto the futon and decide to stay there for a while.

stix: Kass? Are you still there?

I have to ignore him.

stix: Kass?

Maybe if I just cover my eyes . . .

stix: I guess you're gone. Maybe some other time. See you around.

Is he still talking?

stix: Hope I didn't upset you or anything. Later. Bye.

He must have gotten the message by now.

* stix has gone offline. *

✳ *Chapter Seven* ✳

Apparently I Need a Warm-up for National Humiliation

It seems like forever before I uncover my eyes, get up from the bed, and look at the screen, but knowing me it's probably seconds. I'm ashamed of how energized I feel, and how much that makes me want to laugh like one of those creepy Tickle Me Elmo toys. It comes out in small bursts that I manage to stifle by clapping both hands over my mouth. I stare at the words *stix has gone offline*, but not hard enough to change them. *Stop it, self!*

I sit back down at the computer and read over the transcript. It's hard not to smile about how well I come across—not too desperate at all, though obviously that was before I knew who he was. Some of his comments almost make the Elmo monster come out again: *So far, so good . . . Lucas said you had a good sense of humor.* I always assumed it would feel like an insult for a boy to like me for my jokes—meaning that he thought I had a face like a warthog—but by the feel of the absurd grin on my face I've obviously changed my mind.

It's not often I volunteer to go into Raff's room, but he has to be the key to how the Other Cass got my screen name.

"Raff, can I come in?"

"What for?"

"Just need to ask you something."

"Ask me from there."

"Come on, Raff, it'll only take a second." The calm in my voice impresses me—I usually turn feral at the first hint of Raff being difficult, but being serene, like Mom always is with him, seems to have done the trick, because I hear him come toward the door. Then I hear the sound of him trying to turn a key without making a sound.

"When did you get a key cut?" I say.

"*Sssshhh*. What do you want?" He opens the door enough for me to see half his face.

"Let me in."

"No way."

"Let me in or I'll tell Dad you've got a key for your room."
Bingo.

"So, I've just been speaking to someone named *stix* on IM."

"Who?"

"Stix. As in drum. Come on, Raff. I know you gave my screen name to Cassian."

"Who, Luke's brother? Why would *he* want it?"

"I don't know. Oh, come on already, you gave it to him, didn't you? What did he say? Did he ask you about me?"

"You wish, Kass." Forget Protective Services, what's the

number I dial when I'm being emotionally battered by my thirteen-year-old brother? "Oh, wait, I did give it to Lucas, though."

"You *what*?"

"Chill. He paid me twenty bucks for it. I'll give you ten percent."

How I wish I was quick enough to do that math. Having all the scruples and none of the brains is a raw deal.

"I don't want your money. You can't just *sell* information about me. That's sick."

"Everything is for sale, Kass. Get real."

I don't know what's bothering me more: the fact that Raff is profiting from his friend's sad little crush on me, or the thought that it was Lovelorn Lucas on IM all along, pretending to be his much more eligible brother. I need to read the transcript again.

Raff is just about to close the door when I manage to jam my foot in the gap. It hurts a lot more than it looks like it does on TV.

"Ow! So you're saying Cassian has never asked about me, is that right?"

He smiles and shrugs. I have a flashback to belting him over the head with my Barbie (after he'd shaved off all her hair and drawn on tattoos), and make my way back up to my room before I do something I'll regret.

If Monday was confusing, Tuesday is suspicious. When I wake I'm dubious of the time showing on my alarm clock; I feel as if I've only had a couple of hours' sleep. I get dressed and open my bedroom door, but as soon as I'm on the landing I have to go back into the room and check in the full-length mirror that I haven't forgotten anything crucial. Like pants. (St. Agatha's moved into the twenty-first century last year with the advent of pants as an option. With legs like mine that was a minor triumph. Not to mention the whole feminist argument. Win-win!)

I smell the milk three times before pouring it on my cereal. Dad comes into the kitchen and just smiles before getting himself another coffee. He's up to something else. He's talked about the audition at every available opportunity since Saturday, and now he's silent. It's shark-size fishiness, and possibly just as treacherous.

Mom kisses the side of my head as she passes by, gathering up keys, purse, and jacket. She smells different. I bet her boss has ordered her to change her perfume. Or maybe she's always smelled that way and it's my olfactory nerve that's playing up (we learned about that in Biology the other day—you can tell it's recent information by the very fact that I've retained it. Give it another week and I'll be asking Olfactory Who?)

On the bus my Virtually Aimless Brain Zigzag is dizzying. It's as if I'm two people. I'm the misjudged friend, trying to figure out how she's hurt the nicest person she knows and anxious to make things good again. But then I'm a girl thinking of a boy, thinking of his boots and the way he could just about tuck his hair behind one ear, and thinking of the words on the screen that mean he might just like me, too. If I could stay two people, maybe I could make the boy two people as well. Then Char could dream about her Dream Boy, and I could dream about the Other Cass. They are already different people in my head. Almost.

When Izzy gets on I realize how desperate I am to tell someone about the IM conversation last night, and about my suspicion that it may have been Lucas instead of his brother. To put it mathematically—which I wouldn't usually do, except the chaos of the situation seems to be calling for something pragmatic—I'm 65 percent sure it was the Other Cass. More important, I'm 35 percent doubtful.

"Hi. How was Char last night?" I say.

Izzy shrugs, and then breathes out heavily as if she hasn't exhaled for hours. *Why* do people keep *shrugging* at me?

"Izz, I wouldn't ever *do* anything, you know. I love Char."

"I know. Anyway, it's not as if he even likes you, right? It's just that Char has had a thing for him for so long. It's weird how much it's affected her."

I'm nodding, though I feel suddenly very far away and wounded by Izzy's perfectly reasonable statement: *It's not as if he even likes you.* I feel so silly.

"So why don't you just say you're sorry, swear on your life you'll never go out with him, and we can all get back to normal."

"Fine."

"Excellent. We're nearly at her stop. So, how's your dad? Any more weirdness? Have you talked about songs yet?"

I know Izzy's talking, I know she's expecting me to answer, but my internal hard drive is frozen.

"Kass?"

"It's not fine, actually."

"Oh, God, what now? Honestly, all this conflict is giving me a headache." She pinches the bridge of her nose the way I've seen her mom do a lot.

"Is it? Because you seemed to enjoy it yesterday."

"*Enjoy* it? What are you talking about?"

I'm not sure. But now that it's out I feel compelled to continue.

"Just the way you sided with Char right away."

"What? I didn't side with her. She was upset."

"*I* was upset!"

"What about?"

How weak would it sound if I said, "I don't know"? But I don't, I just know that whatever words are coming out of my mouth now feel true.

"Let's just forget it," I say.

"You can't say that now."

"Well, I just did."

"God, talk about extremes."

Ouch.

That settles it—I decide to keep to myself for the rest of the day. See how they like being frozen out like they're doing to me.

Before we're dismissed for the day, Mrs. Roach, our homeroom teacher, says she's got some information she's sure we'll be glad to stay behind for. Knowing her, it'll be about math tutoring or being in the spring musical. You'd think with the amount of time teachers spend in the company of teenagers, they'd have a better handle on what makes us tick.

"This Friday there will a disco at St. Joseph's."

Excuse-me-hello-what? A social, nonacademic event involving St. Agatha's girls and St. Joseph's boys in the same room? At the same time? I may even gloss over the fact that Mrs. Roach said the word *disco*. For now.

"The event will raise money for Save the Children—"

Here comes the part where she ruins it by telling us we all have to wear red noses while we "boogie."

"—and the main attraction will be the karaoke machine!"

Thud. That was the sound of my head falling to my desk. Karaoke is the very last thing I need in my life.

"In fact, a very kind St. Agatha's parent has agreed to organize our very own version of *The X Factor*. There'll be judges and voting and a really spectacular prize for the winner. So if everyone could . . ."

Mrs. Roach's voice fades into the background as a miniature of my dad doing his Gollum impression leaps onto my desk. *It's you, isn't it, Dad? This unspeakable event has got your name all over it.* Gollum scuttles into his cave, muttering, "The winner you will be, my precious, Gollum will fix that. . . ."

This is bad.

The *X Factor* audition seemed far away, not to mention far-fetched, and totally separate from my life at school—the next horrible thing I had to do for my dad, to keep what happened back in December *back in December* as opposed to returning to haunt us. Behind closed doors.

But now this "disco" is three days away in a church hall up the road, and people I know will be there. Plus people I don't know. People! In public! And now the rest of my week will be tied up with Dad nagging me about songs and looks and self-confidence and aiming high and the right food and the right attitude and potential and talent and the whole freakin' pot of delusionary gold at the end of the goddamn rainbow.

No wonder he was so quiet this morning; I'd feared it was the start of another GTD, but no, he was just conserving energy to ruin my life even more.

Rapid thaw required: I need my friends right now. Spoonfuls of sympathy like warm caramel sauce from Char, and nuggets of practical advice like vitamin pills from Izzy.

"Char, Izzy—I'm sorry." I get a smile from Izz and a one-armed shrug from Char. "Char, he was just there for a second. I couldn't even pick him out of a lineup of people who don't actually look like him—that's how significant the whole thing was. I didn't like him—I mean, not that he wasn't nice, he was, just not my type—and he *definitely* didn't look twice at me. He was looking at the TV the whole time. And anyway, Char, I would never, ever do anything to hurt you. Cassian is off-limits. Friends come first."

Suddenly Char throws herself at me and cries something into my blazer that eventually becomes audible:

"Sorry, Kass. It's not you, it's . . . sorry, Kass."

Izzy gives us a triumphant therapist beam.

"Oh, no, your blazer." Char sniffles the remains of what's now smeared on my shoulder and tries to wipe me with her sleeve.

"It's fine. Don't worry."

"Sorry for being so . . ."

"Don't worry," I say. She looks so sweet, all tearstained and happy again, which makes the nagging feeling I have — that this isn't at all over — feel like poison.

∗ *Chapter Eight* ∗

Why Have One Totally Weird Parent
When You Can Have Two?

Both of my elbows are resting on red apples; my head rests in my hands. It's dinnertime, and the suspicion that's been gnawing away at me all day has split open with Mrs. Roach's earth-shattering announcement. As Izzy would say, *better out than in* (and she doesn't mean gas—as if Izzy would ever advocate farting). So now the proverbial boil is lanced (I think I read that in Shakespeare last semester), and I just need to deal with the pus. (I did say it was dinnertime, didn't I? Maybe I'll forget about the pus until afterward.)

The way Dad plunks himself down at the table next to me, all breathless and smiling as if he's just sprinted here from his Life-Wrecking Laboratory, makes me desperate to fling him a sarcastic line about Friday night, but I've already decided not to involve Mom and Raff. This time I'm going to try a calm, serious talk, just Dad and me.

I need sustenance first.

Nobody speaks when Mom puts dinner on the table. We look at the plates, then at one another, then at the plates again, then at Mom, who is winding spaghetti carbonara around her fork.

"Another bad day, hon?" says Dad.

"Hmm?"

"We had spaghetti carbonara *last* night," says Raff.

"Oh, did we?"

Mom keeps on eating as if she hasn't for days. As for the rest of us, our forks are hovering but not yet committing.

"If you don't like it," she says, "just eat the salad." She doesn't sound angry, and she isn't apologizing in that *Stepford Wives* way that used to make me cringe. She's just very matter-of-fact, and clearly *very* hungry. I like it. I'm also horrified by the thought of how empty I'd be if I just ate salad, so I dig my fork in and eat with the same enthusiasm.

"It's good, Mom," I say. I think that's a smile but she doesn't look at me—she's busy piling green salad onto her plate and folding huge lettuce leaves through her wide-open lips, which are now wet with salad dressing and chewing eagerly. A fascinating creature.

"I'm out again tonight," she says with her last mouthful. She clears away her plate while the rest of us are still plowing through our meals. "Have to do a few things for you-know-who."

"I've got a lot to do, anyway," says Dad. He winks at me; I scowl. Mom keeps going as if she hasn't heard him. We chew and chew as she puts on her coat, leaves the room, comes back in with her head half in her bag, looks in the general direction of the table, and swings around as she says, "See you later."

At the click of the front door, all's very still.

"What was that about?" I say. Dad and Raff munch seriously, strands of spaghetti swinging from their lips. I take an unsubtle look underneath the table and see that Raff's right hand is typing (he's probably remortgaging the house). Dad's legs are jiggling. I wonder if they even noticed how un-Mom-like Mom seemed.

"I've got to talk to you about something," says Dad. "There's this little thing on Friday I've sort of organized."

I start gulping down water to wash back what I really want to say about that.

"It's nothing to get worked up about, Kassidy, I just want you to, um, *sing* at this small party I've planned. Consider it like an . . . an open rehearsal."

"Dad, can we talk about this later?"

"Why wait? Seize the moment! I've written down a few songs I think you could do. It'd be the perfect dry run—all your friends there, cheering you on."

I'm trying really hard to stay calm, but what's the point if it's just not working?

"I've highlighted the ones I think we should practice tonight. No calls or TV, OK, Kassidy? I don't want any of your nonsense on this."

I can feel it all bubbling inside me, carbonara about to curdle.

"We'll talk hair and wardrobe tomorrow—I want to steer

you away from this grungy look you've adopted. Fresher, Kassidy! Pretty! You look so depressing sometimes."

OK, that does it.

"I'm *not* doing it." I smack an apple. "I can't believe you've organized this behind my back, to begin with. I can't believe you expect me to do something that makes me feel physically sick. And I don't even know why I can't believe it, because you are *always* pulling crap like this on me."

"Kassidy, please—"

"Why can't you just let me be ordinary?" I stand up, clutching the salad bowl and my half-full plate, walk away from Dad's horror-struck face, and let the dishes clatter into the sink. I'm shaking, and all the muscles in my back feel like they're being pulled into a central point by wire.

"You're not ordinary, Kassidy."

"I am, to *everyone* but you. I don't see Mom jumping up and down about my many 'talents,' and Raff certainly doesn't think I'm anything special."

"It's true, I don't," says the boy with one finger up his nose.

"See, Dad? So *why* can't you just drop all of this and just let me be . . . *me?*"

He's like a chameleon. Just a second ago he looked like an overbearing bully, declaring his agenda, no questions asked. Now he looks like a child who's just learned that he's landed on Santa Claus's naughty list this year. I turn around to face the sink again but it's no good; I can see him reflected in the window.

"As entertaining as this is, I've got stuff to do," says Raff, and against the inky sky I see the tiny figure of my brother going upstairs to get on with his life of crime in peace. Dad's been quiet a long time. I dare to hope that he might actually have heard me.

"Kassidy, this will be the last thing, I promise. I just know I'm right about you—you're *not* ordinary. I'm so, so excited about this. I haven't felt like this for . . . look! Look at my hands, I'm shaking with the buzz of this!"

Against my better judgment I turn and look. He is.

"I tell you what, Kassidy—I'll e-mail you the songs I've been thinking of, and you can go upstairs, go through them, and see which one feels right. Then come down and we'll get to work. OK? That's fair."

He reaches across the table to my cell phone, which I oh-so-stupidly left on the table, but his hand stops just short of picking it up. He looks up at me with his impish grin.

"I'll leave that there."

He pats it and leaves.

I could scream. He's like an 18-wheeler with no brakes, tearing around a racetrack honking its horn—it's all about this great big truck, nothing else on the track matters, around and around, and I'm driving in the opposite direction, but every time we're heading for a collision I swerve out of the way. I don't want him to keep going around, but I can't let him crash.

In my room, I sit with the lights out. I'm on my bed in the dark underneath the cooing and the patter of rain, as far away from my computer as possible. In a room this size it means I can still smell it. Every muscle in my body is being used to fully resist logging on. In contrast, it takes zero effort to resist reading the e-mail Dad will have sent.

I dial half of Izzy's number. Hang up. I dial half of Char's and wait for the robo-woman to tell me that the number I have dialed is incomplete. *Please try again.* I know that this fight with Char felt worse because it was our first, but now I wonder if I really know her, or her me. In a million years I wouldn't have been able to predict the way she's been with me this week. And the way she was behaving, it's as if she thinks I'm some kind of Professional Boyfriend Stealer. It's ridiculous—I have absolutely no powers where boys are concerned. I'm a Professional Boyfriend Repellent—I think I was born with an invisible garlic bulb around my neck.

Rehearsal in Dad's study is exhausting. Maybe it really would be better to be one of those people who think they can sing when they can't. I would rather listen to anything else: nails down a blackboard, retching, someone hawking up loads of phlegm and then spitting it out, *anything*. Unfortunately the look on Dad's face is very "Hark! The Herald Angels Sing!"

I just do what I have to do to keep him quiet, and afterward I'm too stressed out for anything but sleep.

– *Hang on, we've seen you before, haven't we? Katie Something-or-other.*
– *Kass Kennedy.*

– Sounds like a speech impediment. Anyway, what brings you back?

– My dad wants me to audition again, Mr. Cowell.

– Your dad? Oh, give me strength. I am so bored of parents plunking their talentless children in front of me and begging me to make them stars. Have you got star quality, Katie?

– I don't think so, no.

– So why don't you just tell your dad you'd rather not come here night after night wasting my time? Hmm?

– Well, I'm worried about what he might do.

– Do? What, to me? Look, you know I have bodyguards—I can call them in anytime; they're huge, and they can—

– Calm down, Mr. Cowell. He's not going to touch you. He's not like that. He sort of . . . turns in on himself. He folds up, shuts down, whatever you want to call it. If I say no, it's like I'm pushing down the lid on a jack-in-the-box: He's going down and down, you can see he doesn't want to, and then he's gone, and you're left there just waiting for the next moment he'll pop up, only you're not sure he ever will.

– Er, right. Very deep. You mean he's a fruit loop.

– No! Don't talk about him like that.

– OK, OK, I'm sorry. Back to business, seeing as I'm stuck with you. So, if you haven't got star quality, what other qualities have you got?

– Umm . . .

– Today, preferably, darling.

– Sorry, Mr. Cowell. Well, I'm a good friend.

– Really? That's not what I heard. I heard you couldn't stop thinking about Char's boyfriend, and that even now that you're fast asleep you're just itching to go online to chat with stix again.

– But I didn't. I haven't. And he's not her boyfriend.

– Yes, yes — you didn't. Yet. But it's the wanting to, isn't it, Katie?

– Is it, Mr. Cowell?

– I'm afraid so, darling. Now, are you going to sing me something or not? Preferably nothing to do with fish sticks this time.

– How about "Anytime You Need a Friend"?

– I don't think so.

– OK, "You've Got a Friend in Me"?

– Absolutely not.

– I can sing the theme song from Friends if you like.

– Fine, give it a whirl, whatever.

. . .

– Well, go on, then!

. . .

– Oh, marvelous — chaps, she's wet herself again. Someone get her off. . . .

✳ Chapter Nine ✳

What Has Four Wheels, Two Eyes, and Makes My Heart Go Thumpety-Thump?

Sometimes when life accelerates you get so used to the new speed that it's a jolt when it slows down to normal. When I woke on Wednesday morning my mind was still racing, but Wednesday was covered in speed bumps: complicated math class, Izzy's latest argument with her dad (about her mom, naturally), and Raff sitting next to someone at the bus stop who was eating KFC. There wasn't time for anything else.

Dad orders Indian takeout in the evening because Mom has to drive her best friend Maria to a Pilates class, because Maria's husband is abroad and Maria's car has broken down. Mom goes into great detail about Maria's husband and the trip and the mechanical problems of the Volkswagen Jetta, and I can tell we all want to say, "So what?" at some of the trivia but we don't. I suspect it's because Mom so rarely talks for that long at a time that we are pretty curious as to what was going to come out. Who would have guessed it'd be Maria's oil pump?

Amazingly, Dad doesn't talk about the Unholy Mess that is Friday night's "disco," but he doesn't have to because it's all there, simmering away under my skin. He eats like he's fueling himself for something big. Raff takes a naan, plunks a load of lamb korma in the middle, and folds it over so he can eat it one-handed. I eat slowly but steadily, almost rhythmically, like I've been programmed.

Soon the curry's gone, unless you count the onions in the sauce at the bottom of the container, or the little container of onion chutney we're never sure what to do with, or the half-eaten potato-onion pakora. I wonder how many onion trees are pointlessly decimated just to end up in people's trash cans, until I remember that onions don't grow on trees.

Raff says, "Dad, Lucas is coming over in a sec because we're doing a joint project."

Was I just thinking about onions? Lucas is coming over!

"That's nice. What's the project?" says Dad.

Who cares! When is he coming, Raff? He can't be coming alone, not at thirteen years old and in the dark, can he?

"It's on the . . . Brazilian rain forest."

Of course it is, Raff. Very convincing.

"Sounds good. Do we need to pick him up and drop him off, though, since Mom's got the car?"

Someone else is dropping him off, Raff, aren't they? *Aren't they?* Speak, boy!

"I think someone else is dropping him off."

Suddenly I'm thinking about onions again, only now it's

the worry of whether I smell of them, and about that pallid, swollen look I get when I've just stuffed my face. On the other hand, repelling him with onions might be exactly what a true friend would do.

I clear away the takeout rubble and find myself wiping down the apples with antibacterial Windex. In the sitting room I smack each cushion and throw them back on the sofa casually until they look exactly right. The newspapers go in one pile on the coffee table; the remote control goes on the arm of the sofa; I kick my clunky school shoes behind a giant potted plant.

"What are you doing?" says Raff.

"Nothing."

"Yeah, right. Anyway, Dad wants you in his study."

"Why should I? I'm not going to his stupid 'disco.' It's not fair; it's so embarrassing; I just can't." It's unclear who I'm appealing to. The giant potted plant, perhaps?

"Whatever, Kass," says my ever-supportive brother. "But just so you know . . . oh, but I'm sure you're not interested. I'll just keep it to myself."

"Know what? Come on."

"Nah, never mind, you wouldn't be interested."

At the sound of our doorbell I run up to my room two stairs at a time, nearly stumble backward at the top, and have to clutch the banister. I crouch there, trying to catch my breath but having to hold it so I can make out the voices downstairs. I can hear my dad, though not exactly what he's saying; they must still have the front door open and the sound is traveling out the wrong way.

By the tone of his voice I know he's not talking to either Raff or Lucas.

The front door closes. I run into my parents' room and wrestle with the sheer curtains, trying to reach the window. A figure walks to a little yellow car. I've opened the window before I have any idea what to say, and it's not exactly the sort of weather for randomly opening windows.

"Hi," I call out, and then duck back inside and contemplate stuffing my mouth with curtain.

"Kass?"

Oh, God, it is definitely him.

"Yeah, hi. I was just looking out for my friend."

"Cool. I just dropped off my brother. So, how are you?" He walks closer, hands in pockets. He's wearing the brown boots again. Not for my benefit, obviously.

"Yeah, awesome, thanks." Awesome? Never has a word been more uncool.

"Good, because I was worried I'd offended you the other night." He kicks the curb and nearly stumbles, and then kicks it again as he recovers. The goofiness is even more appealing than the boots.

"Offended me? Oh, no way, not at all. I just had to go."

"OK. That's good, I mean."

More curb kicking. I hope I'm far enough away so that he can't hear my teeth chattering; it's so cold and I'm only in my school shirt. I hear a cat and very nearly start a conversation about the terrible yowling noise they make when they're in heat. Thank God he speaks first.

"I'm supposed to be studying but I feel like going for a drive."

"Sounds good. I like your little car."

Rewind. *Rewind*. He'll think you want to go for a drive with him. And should I have referred to his car as *little*?

"Too bad you can't come along."

I can't? Should I remember why I can't?

"But have a nice time with your friend. See you, Kass."

Oh, that's right, I'm leaning out of this window waiting for my friend. *Stupid, stupid friend.*

"Yeah, see you, Cass."

He walks to his little yellow car and puts the key in the lock.

"Guess I'll see you Friday," he says, getting in but leaving one long leg on the curb.

"Really? Why's that?"

"I'm one of the bouncers for that party. Your dad asked me."

GIRL ASPHYXIATES SELF WITH SHEER CURTAIN.

"Oh, right! Awesome, that's . . . *awesome*."

GIRL FOUND FACEDOWN IN VERY SHALLOW POOL OF ENTHUSIASM.

"He said you were going to be singing."

"That's the plan. Dad's plan, that is. I'm not exactly very good."

GIRL CRUSHED TO DEATH BY MASSIVE UNDERSTATEMENT.

"I bet you're just being modest. My band might do the *X Factor* thing, too. Just talked with your dad about it—he's a cool guy, figures we should all just go for it. He's so positive, you know?"

What is my dad up to now? Is he going to lead the entire population of local teenagers down to the X Factor *auditions like the Pied Piper?*

"Um, I guess that's one word for it. He can be kind of a pain."

"Yeah, well, what would I know? He's your dad. I haven't even seen mine since I was two."

GIRL SMASHES SKULL AFTER TOPPLING OUT OF SECOND-FLOOR WINDOW WHILE TRYING TO RETRIEVE PREVIOUS SENTENCE.

"Oh! Sorry."

"Not your fault." He smiles and shrugs. "Anyway, I thought it'd be cool knowing someone else who's going to audition."

GIRL RECONSIDERS SUICIDE PACT WITH SELF.

"It would, yeah . . . what? What are you laughing at? What's funny?"

"Sorry, sorry, nothing. You're kind of weird, Kass—nice weird, I mean."

He thinks I'm nice? He thinks I'm weird? He thinks I'm something?

GIRL DECIDES SUICIDE DEFINITELY OUT FOR NOW.

"Thanks, I guess." Thank God I don't say, *You're nice, too.*

"You're nice, too."

No!!!! Recover! Recover!

"Um, I'd better save my voice. Night air and stuff."

"OK, bye then, Kass. See you Friday." Wow. There should be some sort of government health alert on his smile. Warning: May cause loss of morals.

"Friday. OK. Bye."

Suddenly I freak out about the sheer curtains draped on my shoulders looking suspiciously like a bridal veil, so I shake them off and close the window as he draws his leg into the little yellow car. He's gone up the street and I'm heading for my room and I have

Absolutely

No

Idea

What to Do.

✳ *Chapter Ten* ✳

Attack of the Killer Conscience

I get through that evening's rehearsals with Dad by being somewhere else—*ish*. My body is in Dad's office, making some pretty inhuman sounds, but my mind is outside in the street with the Other Cass. I keep going over the same imaginary scene: I open the front door and he's standing there, hands in his pockets, head to the side and a killer smile. He puts his arm around me as we walk toward his little yellow car (I seem to be draped in a sheer curtain). But then we stop—something's not right. Either I say something stupid or I trip over his brown boots or the car turns into a giant banana. So then back I go to the front door and replay the whole thing.

"Are you OK, Kassidy?" says Dad. "You seem . . . distracted."

"I'm just visualizing," I say. Which is not a lie.

"Good girl. Only, try not to visualize when you're actually performing because you get a kind of dopey expression when you do it. OK?"

"Fine. Is this over now? I'm tired."

"We should really do another—"

"My voice, Dad; I mean *my voice* is tired. It's not good to strain it, you know that."

"Sorry, you're right—I'll get you a glass of salt water to take up with you."

As I log in to IM, the last of the salt crystals sinks to the bottom of the glass, but nothing about me feels settled. I almost can't look at the screen in case he's there.

He's there!

I'll pretend I haven't seen him. If I sit here and chat with someone else, or Google *something*—I'm sure I need to Google something—there's no harm done, is there?

stix: Hello

It'd be rude not to say hello. Just hello, and then I'll make an excuse.

curlygirl: hi
stix: Nice time with your friend?
curlygirl: yes thanks
stix: What else you been doing?
curlygirl: not much
stix: You OK? Don't seem very chatty. Want me to go?

Here it is: the perfect way to get rid of him. Say you're tired, say you have studying to do, say you're going to take a bath — no, don't say bath or he might think you're trying to make him think about you naked!

curlygirl: dont go. sorry was just distracted by something but am ok now

Interesting. Still, I suppose a quick IM wouldn't hurt. I could even find out some stuff about him to tell Char. Think of it as a favor to a friend.

curlygirl: did u go for drive?

stix: Quick one, went to see a friend.

curlygirl: someone in ur band?

stix: Used to be. There was a big fight about him and he got kicked out.

curlygirl: oh. why, wasn't he good enough? what did he play?

stix: Bass. He's a genius. But he's got ADHD and it pissed everyone off.

curlygirl: doesn't seem v fair. why?

stix: Complicated. He's just harder to be with, I guess, than most other people — well, that's what they thought. It's not what I think.

curlygirl: hard how?

stix: Lots of things that "normal" (whatever they are) people do, Tom does, too, only all the time — like forgetting rehearsal, or interrupting a lot, fidgeting, kind of wired, like he's powered by some kind of superfuel that he's not completely in charge of. I dunno, I'm probably not explaining it well. But he's cool. I like him a lot and felt bad for not being able to convince the others to keep him.

curlygirl: sounds like u did ur best. u can't make people understand sometimes

stix: Sounds like you've been there.

How has it come to this? I want to tell him about Dad. Should I? Why *would* I?

stix: Uh-oh, silence. Sorry, was that too personal? ☹
curlygirl: no is fine, sorry! just thinking
stix: About . . . ?
curlygirl: ur friend. i dont talk about this much, so swear u wont tell?
stix: I swear. On my drumsticks ☺
curlygirl: ☺ ok well its about my dad. he's got a disorder, kind of like ur friend. not the same though. something different

I can't believe I'm telling him. It feels dangerous, but it feels right.

stix: Do you know the name of it?
curlygirl: yep. cyclothymic disorder. thats what we think anyway

stix: I haven't heard of it.

curlygirl: have u heard of bipolar?

stix: Beethoven had that.

curlygirl: oh didnt know that! isnt britney s supposed 2 have it?

stix: Britney and Beethoven—who knew they had so much in common??

curlygirl: ☺ anyway my dad doesnt have that but its like a mild form of it. it can turn into bipolar. thats what we worry about. a lot

stix: How likely is that?

curlygirl: idk. i must sound really stupid but dont know much more about it

stix: You don't sound stupid at all. Must be really hard. Is he in treatment for it?

curlygirl: no. he wont. gets scared when hes really low—like scared of everything—but then when hes up doesn't think anything wrong at all. hes in an up cycle now = so enthusiastic he could levitate. thats how x factor stuff got started

stix: You mean you don't want to do it?

curlygirl: ☹

stix: Seems harsh. What would happen if you just said no?

This is getting too hard. I've said enough. I feel like crying.

stix: Kass? Are you still there?

stix: Your dad seems really nice. Must be difficult. Don't be upset.

curlygirl: he'll be ok. i'd better go

stix: Really? Stay—we can talk about something else. Anything: particle physics, organometallic compounds, crystallography . . .

curlygirl: i could talk at length about any of those. r u a geek?

stix: Sshh. Swear you won't tell.

curlygirl: i swear. on ur drumsticks

stix: ☺ Are you sure your boyfriend won't mind you staying up all night talking to me?

Dilemma: Do I tell the Other Cass that I've never ever ever in my fifteen long years had a whiff of a boyfriend? Or . . .

curlygirl: actually i broke up with someone a while ago. he was a jerk. immature. anyway back to particle physics

An hour later I finally say good night to the Other Cass. I log out, and then print our entire conversation and shove it in my desk drawer. My eyes ache from staring at the screen so long, or maybe my treachery is turning me blind.

I lie on my bed, spread out like a starfish. My mind is whirring, so I concentrate hard to make everything get in line: First I wonder if I would have gone for a drive with him if I hadn't inadvertently turned down the invitation by mentioning the mysterious Friend. Then I wonder how I would have convinced my dad to let me. Then I wonder why on earth someone like him is asking someone like me to get into his little yellow car, or talking to me all night on IM. Then I wonder how the hell I'm going to get through Friday night. Then I wonder why I'm even contemplating going now. *Especially* now that he's going to be there. Then I wonder what it means that I could tell the Other Cass about my dad but I don't even talk about it with my best friends. Then I think of Char.

She shouldn't be that far down the list. Char deserves better. So what if I've already had more of a conversation with him than she's managed in four years? So what if it's him flirting with me and leaving his long leg hanging out of the little yellow car door as if it's in any way possible not to like it? And who cares if he's the only guy I've felt this loopy over who's ever shown a flicker of an eyelash of interest in me?

It's like a sickness. This must be what they mean by two-faced, because I really feel like two people at the moment. There's probably some psychological term for it that Izzy could enlighten me with, only something tells me I can't trust Izzy with this new information. I have a pretty good idea which side of the fence she'd stand on. Because there is a fence, I have to admit. It's gnarled and ugly and I'll get splinters in my butt cheeks if I sit on it much longer.

I'm so far into my thoughts that I almost don't notice when my phone screen lights up.

CHAR CALLING

"Hello?"

"Hey, Kass."

"Hey. Are you OK? You don't usually call me in the evening."

"Oh, I'll hang up, then."

"No! I didn't mean that. I just wondered if you were OK."

"I guess so. You?"

"Yep, I'm fine."

This is a nightmare. I can't think of a single thing to say to her.

"So what's going on at your place tonight?" she says.

"Usual. Dad's plotting my downfall. Mom's out with her friend Maria, which at least is a change from running errands for her boss. You know what he's like: 'Get me a Triple Thick Wheatgrass Shake Squeezed by the Silken-Covered Feet of Albino Shetland Ponies.' He's always on some health kick that Mom has to cater to."

"Yeah, sure. So she'll be out all evening?"

"Um, yeah, although I guess she could be back by now—I've been in my room."

"OK."

"Doing homework."

"OK."

"Yeah, *Death of a Salesman* essay."

"OK. I have to go, actually."

"Uh, OK. Are you all right, Char?"

"Yep. Bye, Kass."

When she hangs up, tears sting my eyes and I have a horrible premonition about what it would feel like if that were our last ever conversation. Was it Char who was being super-weird just then, or was it me? My nana always says you should never let the sun go down on an argument, but what about the day after an argument—your first argument—when things are still strained and you've just had a bizarro conversation about your Mom's boss and your English homework?

I call her back.

Voice mail. Only it's Char's dad's voice, which doesn't make leaving a message any easier.

"You've reached Charlotte's voice mail. Leave a brief message with your name and number."

"Char, it's Kass again. Bit crazy, 'cause I know we just got off the phone but . . . are you all right? Um, sleep well. See you tomorrow, babe."

It's suddenly simple. It's my kind, always-there-for-me friend, who hardly ever complains (even about her Sergeant Major Dad, though Izzy and I both know what a control freak he is) and puts her friends first and hasn't had a single whiff of luck since her mom left without so much as a good-bye note versus Some Boy.

No contest. Char means way more to me. This was all just a blip—a distraction from the real problem in my life: Dad.

✳ *Chapter Eleven* ✳

Have Myself a Merry Little Christmas Dessert

We're in our usual formation on the bus; Char has just joined us. Her cheeks were icy when she kissed us hello, and now she blows warm air into her cupped hands and rubs them. She hasn't smiled yet but I suspect it's just the cold. Anyway, I'm about to tell her something that will really take her mind off the weather.

"Guess what, Char?"

"What?" She doesn't look at me but hunches her shoulders and shivers and cups her hands again. I don't remember it being *that* cold outside.

"I know where a certain someone is going to be tonight."

"Who?"

I just grin at her and nod.

"You mean . . . ?" She gasps; I think she gets it.

"Yep. He's coming to the karaoke."

Izzy shoots me a worried glance, not knowing that I'm about

to make everything all right, and Char springs to life — the slightly hyper side of life.

"He's not. Is he? Why is he? Why would he? Oh, my God. My dad even said I could go. Oh, my God. Is he really?"

"Let's just calm down," says Izzy. She takes one of Char's thin pink hands from the bus seat and rubs it between hers.

"I just found out," I lie. "Lucas came over to see Raff, and I overheard them saying that Cassian had been asked to be a doorman." Another lie, but for the best, I figure.

"But isn't your dad organizing this thing? How come he didn't tell you?" says Izzy. Who is she, Veronica Mars?

"Dad's just organizing the actual karaoke, I think. Anyway, Cassian hasn't been over again so I don't know when Dad could have asked him. So it couldn't have been. Dad, I mean." Strike three. I really hope that's enough lies to cover it up so that Char can just enjoy the information rather than wondering where it came from.

"I feel sick," she says. "I can't go."

"Don't be silly, Char. This is your chance," I say.

"Really? Will you help me? I mean, come home with me after school, help me get ready, just . . . *please*, Kass, you have to *help* me."

She looks like she's facing a leg amputation. Apparently I'm the anesthetic.

"Wouldn't Izzy be better? She's much calmer than me, and better at makeup." (OK, that really *is* a lie. Izzy's a natural beauty, which is lucky because she puts makeup on like Lady Gaga in the dark.)

"I've got therapy," says Izzy.

"And I *need* therapy," says Char. "Please, Kass."

"Umm, OK. Of course." She doesn't notice the hesitation in my voice, but it's because I haven't brought my took-me-three-hours-to-choose outfit with me, and I usually spend some time on my own before an ordeal like karaoke—I'm better that way. I can't let her down now, though. This could be all I need to fix the weirdness between us for good.

Everyone's talking about tonight. The fact that we're getting worked up about an evening with St. Joe's boys shows just how sparse social events are. All work and no play makes St. Agatha's girls . . . well, *desperate*, by the sounds of it. Boys who spit at the bus stop are suddenly given Hollywood status. Boys who have been known to crumble an entire bag of potato chips and empty it down the back of your school shirt suddenly have "really good bone structure" and "nice hands." Char just smiles. I bet I know what she's thinking; I bet it's the same thing I'm thinking. Only she's allowed to. Those boys are nothing compared to the Other Cass. It almost makes it more romantic that I'm going to help my friend get together with the boy I like. I bet there's a play by Shakespeare about this exact situation. I should read it. Or better still, watch the movie so that I actually have some hope of understanding it.

On the bus ride home I start to fixate on my lack of an outfit. Char sits next to me instead of in front of Izzy, who is penned in by a bald man whose leather jacket smells like Play-Doh.

"Don't worry, you can wear anything of mine," says Char.

"The skinny jeans?" I say.

"Oh."

"I'm kidding, Char. As if I'd even fit into them."

"You would," she insists, very high-pitched.

"OK, I'll wear those."

"Oh."

"Char, I'm KIDDING!"

"Well, stop it, I have no sense of humor in a crisis!" She links arms with me. Izzy shifts around in her seat, trying not to touch Play-Doh Man, and makes an *awww* face. As much as I love Izzy, I wish she wouldn't think she can fix my life all the time. I'm the one who's put Char and me back together. And did she really think I wouldn't know who'd left a pamphlet entitled "Bipolar Parents: What Children Need to Know" in a brown envelope in my locker? Subtle. But I've decided to just ignore it, because I can't deal with another argument with a friend. The pamphlet is tucked into a book in my bag and it can stay there as far as I'm concerned—all I need to know is that I'm about to commit social suicide *and* lose the Boy of Our Dreams on the same night. Enough already. There's no point in having a rug if you can't sweep stuff under it.

"So you're coming straight from therapy, Izz?" I say. Play-Doh Man gives her a little more room and we tut in unison, and then giggle as if that's just further proof that we're so close we're psychic. (Forgetting the recent lapses of power.)

"Therapy, then dinner with Michael, then party," Izzy says. She started calling her dad "Michael" a few weeks ago. She said it was "something I'm trying out."

"Oh, God, you're going to be really late, then," I say.

"Don't worry, I'll be there to watch you pee your pants," she says, deadpan. Play-Doh Man is practically hanging off his seat now. I lightly punch her on the arm.

"Seriously, don't even joke about that. It could happen."

Char giggles. "Is that the time you all went to the audition for crispy pancake mix and they still put your face on the box?" she says.

"Fish sticks," says Izzy, as if she's more of a sushi kind of girl.

"Well, *I* think Kass is going to be a star tonight," says Char. She squeezes my arm and rests her head on my shoulder.

"All the same," says Izzy. She puts her clenched fist toward me and flips it over. Out springs a panty liner.

"Bitch!" I say, but I have to laugh. I have to.

Char and I are both anxious to get to her house without bumping into you-know-who; she doesn't know that, obviously.

"How's your dad been recently?" I say.

"What do you mean?" That was definitely a snap. Things must be difficult with him, poor Char.

"Well, just that he's letting you come tonight. Seems like a good sign." Eggshells: everywhere.

"Probably just wants me out of the house. Anyway, I don't want to talk about him."

"Sure, OK, sorry."

We're at her front door and for the first time I look at the one next to it and have an inkling of who might be inside. I try hard to think of him as Char's Dream Boy again. Only there's the yellow car.

No one greets us as we walk in, and I don't dare mention Char's dad again, but I can't help noticing how different it is to walk into an empty, quiet house. We go straight up to her room. On the way I notice that all the doors are closed.

Char brings her room to life: turns on two lamps, opens the curtains even though it's nearly dark (I wonder if she's looking to see if the yellow car is still there), puts the radio on. I flop onto her bed and kick my shoes off.

"I don't believe it," I say.

"What?"

"The radio."

"Must be a sign," she whispers as the chorus of "Other Side of the World" begins. She hands me a hairbrush. "Come on, then, practice."

"I'm not singing *now*," I say.

"In front of me? You're going to be doing it in front of a church hall full of people in about two hours."

"Let's not talk about it. Can you put something else on?"

She chucks her skinny jeans on the bed and goes to her

computer. She doesn't have much of a music library: Her dad is very particular about what she's allowed to download.

"Bieber?"

"That wholesome little YouTube boy? Sure, Sister Char."

"Shut it or I'll sing the crispy pancake song."

"Fish sticks."

"That too."

We're laughing the way we used to. Now I'm so glad I came back with her. Silly to worry about clothes and my usual rituals; I can find a way to do those here, probably.

"Here, take a look," she says, opening her closet doors. "Anything you want. I mean it."

I'm missing the gene that makes girls totally comfortable about borrowing clothes from their friends, so I automatically choose items from Char's wardrobe that I happen to know she hasn't worn since forever: fitted black long-sleeved T-shirt with a tiny diamanté heart on the right boob, black skinny jeans, thick white belt. I spy some white pointy ankle boots at the bottom. I can't remember ever seeing her in them and I'm too shy to ask if I can wear them, so I "accidentally" spill a whole pile of things out onto the floor so that the boots are just visible.

"Char, what shoes do you think with this outfit?" I hold up the clothes I've chosen.

"Hmm . . . I have those white boots I never wear."

"Which ones . . . these? You think?" OK, I am pathetic, but it's working.

"Definitely. Go for it. Not sure about the belt, though. It's a bit 'outfitty' like that. Black white black white like a zebra, you know?"

"True. No belt. But then isn't it a bit black black white?"

"Ah, yes, but then you wear these." And she hands me a pair of incredible earrings, with shaped and colored beads hanging at different lengths.

"Char, wow, are you sure?"

"'Course. You're my best friend, Kass, and this is a big night for you."

"And you," I say, and her smile is wide and my stomach flips, and I wish we could swap places.

I'm downstairs. There is something very soothing about Char's under-the-stairs bathroom. Is it the beige? The sloping ceiling, maybe, which reminds me of my bedroom. The fact that it is very small in here, a cocoon. It smells of vanilla. There is a corner sink no bigger than a cereal bowl and a round mirror that looks antique. The lighting is low; it catches the beads on the earrings. I look at different parts of my face but not into my eyes.

"Dutch courage," my dad calls this; he's had a shot of something before every one of my auditions. But it's my neck on the line, and this time people I know are going to be there. There is only one bearable outcome of all the possibles: They think my singing is "ironic" and I'm too tipsy to care anyway.

I was worried Char's dad wouldn't have any, but it was at the back of a well-stocked cupboard. I took a miniature Christmas fruitcake as well, to take away the taste, and also because I absolutely love Christmas fruitcake but we never have it at home. I wonder if it's left over from last Christmas or bought early for the next one. As I'm fishing the bottle and the cake out of my backpack, where I'd stashed them in case anyone crept up on me, my copy of *Death of a Salesman* falls out, and with it the pamphlet Izzy planted on me.

Here in the vanilla cocoon I feel compelled to take a quick look.

Chemicals in the brain that are off balance cause bipolar disorder and its related disorders. But we don't know for sure what makes the chemicals go off balance. In some cases, symptoms can appear for no known reason. In other cases, the symptoms seem to come after a life crisis, stress, or illness.

Stress. There it is in black-and-white. And I know what gives Dad stress: me. And I know what makes Dad happy: same answer. So I can do this for him, can't I? I can do a simple thing like sing (terribly) in front of people. How hard could that really be, compared to what he goes through with the chemicals randomly attacking his brain for no good reason? Plus he doesn't even have bipolar . . . yet. Me doing this tiny thing for him might stop that from happening. So what if it's only for now? I'll deal with now first and worry about the rest later.

I decide to read another bit.

Bipolar disorder may also be genetic or inherited. However, it will not usually be passed to children. About one in ten children of a parent with bipolar disorder will develop the illness. Nine out of ten will not.

I shove the pamphlet back in my backpack. Stupid thing. Why did Izzy have to show me this? Suddenly I wish I had listened more in Math class, but one in ten does not sound like good odds to me.

I unscrew the bottle top, pull my sleeve over my hand, and wipe the rim: more a ritual than anything, because I highly doubt that Char's Evil Uptight Dad has been swigging rather than using a glass.

One big gulp of liquid courage later, the burning sensation turns to warm and it's sort of nice in my chest but still icky on my tongue. The Christmas fruitcake is wrapped in silver. It has a tiny plastic holly leaf and two red berries, which I slip into the pocket of Char's black jeans to dispose of later. It tastes so amazing I finish it in four bites. I check my teeth in the mirror and pick out the bits of raisin, then rinse with cold water and my finger and run my tongue around my teeth over and over. I stretch out the muscles in my face and breathe in deeply and look myself in the eye. I'm OK. I'm not crazy. I'm all right.

✳ *Chapter Twelve* ✳

A Kind of Frying Pan–Fire Situation

Dad and I have been texting each other since I left school. He's called sixteen times but I haven't answered. I've read all his messages aloud in a flat, calm voice, so that they couldn't wind me up (as much), and kept my replies brief and firm. Oh, yes, I *would* be going to the party from Char's. And yes, with Char, not him. And no, I would not be wearing the cowboy boots, or the fur-trimmed jacket, or the "bling" (someone needs a vocab overhaul). And yes, I was still set on the "lesbian song." *c u both there*, I ended with. *Just me tonight*, was his final word.

"My mom's not coming," I say to Char as we walk arm in arm to the bus stop.

"Oh. OK." She looks uneasy.

"What's up? Shoes hurting?"

"Yeah. Haven't broken them in yet. I'll be fine."

I'm having trouble in Char's boots, too—my ankles keep

giving way. Can't be the vodka, it was only a drop. I start to giggle as we totter along together.

"You're in a good mood," Char says.

"It's nerves," I reply. She doesn't look in the mood for giggling, so I breathe in the night air to help me stop. "You OK?"

"Yep."

"Worried about seeing Cassian?"

"I wish you wouldn't call him that," she snaps. "You make it sound as if you know him really well now."

"What? I'm just calling him by his name. What else am I supposed to call him?"

She shrugs.

"Sorry, Char. I won't call him that anymore. I'll call him . . ."

"Just don't call him anything."

"OK, OK."

Now that the good vibe between Char and me seems to have disappeared, I'm starting to feel sick with nerves. I was hoping to cover them over with some hypergirly banter on the bus ride, the kind you know must be irritating the hell out of every other passenger but that's so addictive when you're on such a roll that you just don't care. I guess you can't just make that kind of thing happen. At least not when the other person has a face as long as a wet weekend; a wet three-day weekend, even. In prison.

We get on the bus, but it's so crowded that the best we can do are two aisle seats, so now we have that gap between us as well as Char's black mood. I decide to ignore her and go over the lyrics in my head. *Over the sea and . . .*

132

"So why do you think your mom isn't coming?"

"No idea. Probably stuff to do for her boss again." *Over the sea and far away* . . .

"Really? On a Friday night?" There's something really fake about the way Char is asking me these questions.

"Well, the guy's a real nutcase. I told you. He makes all these weird demands."

"Right."

Over the sea and far away, she's waiting like an iceberg . . .

"It's just . . ." She starts again; it's making me extra-jittery. "You'd think she could say no just this one time. I mean, it's a big night for you."

I must be paranoid, but it sounds as if Char is trashing my mom. I've never heard her trash anyone—even her Remote Control Dad when he grounds her for the most trivial thing. Although, come to think of it, I did hear her trash *me* earlier this week. Why is she starting with *my* family? Surely the logical thing is to start with your own and work your way outward.

"It's not really that big. Mom's seen me do this a hundred times. She knows I haven't suddenly developed an amazing talent."

"I guess. Still."

"Still *what?*"

She's seen how stressed I'm getting and something in her changes.

"Nothing. It's nothing. I just think you need support tonight, that's all. I didn't mean anything else."

"OK."

Now there's Char's black mood, an aisle, *and* my black mood between us, and there are too many heads on the bus and the lights are too bright to be able to escape into the view out the window. I press the pointed toes of the white ankle boots together and look down and sing inside my head . . . *fire fades away . . . full of tired excuses . . . too hard to say . . .*

Char links arms with me when we get off the bus. I try not to resent it, but find it hard to drop this little grudge.

"Nervous?" she says.

"A little. You?"

"A little."

We clock him at the same time, and she unlinks arms and stuffs her hands into her jacket pockets, and walks head bowed. He's standing in the entrance, behind Mrs. Roach, who is checking names off a list and collecting the two-dollar fee.

"Nice to see you, girls," says Mrs. Roach, holding out a hand. I'm tempted to high-five it but I give her the cash she's after.

"Hi, Mrs. Roach." Char and I speak in unison as if we're in class, and I cringe at how childish we must sound in front of He Who Must Not Be Mentioned. Assuming he's also He Who Must Not Be Looked At, I pretend to be desperately interested in something over his shoulder and proceed to walk into the hall.

"Hi, you two," he says. I'm not sure whether I should keep on walking, but I don't. I spin around and act surprised.

"Oh, hi! Sorry, I was miles away. Nerves." I'm aware that I'm jiggling like my dad does, as if anyone needs a reenactment of "nerves"—yeah, I think we probably all know what nerves are.

Char is stock-still, right next to him, but looking at me.

"I like your boots," he says.

"Oh, they're Char's," I say. He smiles and nods her way.

"How'd you get here?" he says.

I sense other girls giving us the eye as they walk past our uneasy triangle. It's very much isosceles, which I think is good—Char and Cass close together, and me up here on a faraway point by myself.

"Bus," I say. "We came together from Char's place." Maybe I shouldn't be answering all the questions, but he's looking at me when he asks them.

"Oh, right, I'd have given you a lift if I'd known."

"No worries," I say, hoping I sound as casual as I don't feel. "Anyway, I'd better go in."

"Yeah. Well, I'll see you later," he says. "Good luck, by the way."

Char walks toward me without saying a word to him and grabs my sleeve and pulls me into the hall. She looks intense.

There's a mirror ball spinning from the ceiling and disco lights bouncing off every wall, there's something that sounds disturbingly like seventies music coming full blast from the speakers, and now there's a hissing voice in my right ear.

"I didn't know you were such a good flirt," she says. People's faces come and go: flashes of clothes, shoes, snacks in bowls on long tables.

"I'm not. For God's sake, Char, you didn't say a single word. What was I supposed to do?"

"I couldn't get a word *in*, you mean."

I clutch my head; I can't win here. Am I really that bad?

"What's wrong, Kassidy?" My dad comes rushing over. Just what I need.

"What? Nothing, Dad, why?"

"Your head. Do you have a headache or something?" He looks me over. "You look all patchy."

"Dad, it's the flashing lights. And what is with this music? No one wants this. People will be leaving in droves." Why am I telling him this? I would *love* it if people left in droves.

"This is a classic," he says. He looks upward as if he can see dancing musical notes all around him.

"I like it," says Char. She gives my dad a really weird smile, as if he's a dog holding up a sore paw. Even a dog wouldn't be dumb enough to iron a crease in their jeans, right?

"Thank you, Charlotte. I'm glad someone around here has some taste."

"She's humoring you, Dad," I say. Oh, God, did he put whitener on his running sneakers? Blindfolded?

"Whatever, Kass," says Char. So now my best friend is whatever-ing me? Bring on the karaoke!

Suddenly Dad looks like he's seen a ghost.

"Wow, it's . . . *amazing*."

Char and I look toward the entrance. And there he is.

"Is that . . . ? Dad, what's going on?"

The trousers are high, the chest broad, the T-shirt v-necked, the cleavage hairy. The teeth glow whiter than white underneath the disco lights. Dad walks toward him with both arms outstretched and shakes his hand with the force of a sumo wrestler. For one beautiful moment I think this must *all* be a dream. Correction: nightmare. It may have started in the bathroom at Char's—maybe I drank more than I thought. Or earlier. It may have started the night the Other Cass came over; the night I went to sleep thinking about his leg sticking out of his little yellow car. Or earlier. The night after Char and I had the falling out. Or earlier. Maybe my entire life is a nightmare.

"Pinch me, Char," I say. She does. Really hard, in fact.

"*Ow*. God!"

"You asked for it." She has a point, but . . . *OW*. But I don't have the energy to analyze her disturbing desire to inflict physical pain on me, because my dad is about to introduce me to Simon Cowell.

"Kassidy, allow me to introduce you to Tony."

Who?

"Tony Ferrari—this is my daughter, Kassidy."

"Pleasure, darling." I'm aware that my hand is enclosed by some scarily hairy fingers, and that the fingers lead up an equally hairy arm to a puffed-up chest at my eye level, but I am not at all sure what is going on here.

He is still shaking my hand and making me squint from the glare of his teeth—it looks like Dad used his whitener on those as well.

"Dad? What's . . . who's . . . ?"

"It's good, isn't it?" Dad is openmouthed with glee. With one hand he slaps his thigh and with the other he slaps Simon Cowell on the back. "Tony has come to judge the karaoke. I found him on the Internet. Wow, Tony, uncanny. Thanks for coming."

"Delighted to."

Tony seems to be a man of few words. I like that in a karaoke judge. A simple "tuneless crap" would suit me far better than an in-depth discussion.

"So, you're a look-alike," I say, mainly because I need to confirm it out loud.

"Yes, but I do actually *know* Simon Cowell. I have connections."

"Really?" says Dad, eyes popping out like a toad's.

"Sure. I don't usually talk about it because there are some real weirdos out there, and you never know who's going to try to get closer to Mr. Cowell through me."

Sniff *Smell fish, anyone?*

"This just gets better," says Dad, resuming the thigh slapping.

"How come you're judging karaoke at a school disco, if you don't mind me asking?" I say.

"Kassidy! Don't be rude!" Dad puts his arm around Tony Ferrari. "It's just nerves, Tony, she's not usually so . . . Anyway, come this way and I'll show you to your table. Now then, about these connections . . ."

As Dad leads him away, Tony shoots me what I presume is supposed to be an evil glare straight out of the *Simon Cowell Book of Facial Expressions.* It definitely needs some work. So here I am in a run-down church hall, with a phony judge about to deliver the verdict on an even phonier contestant. Although she's never rescued me yet, I can't help wanting my mom.

It's seven thirty and the place has filled up. St. Agatha's girls stand in small groups and look longingly at St. Joe's boys and the long tables of party food, neither of which we dare approach. The boys, on the other hand, head straight for the food and ignore the girls. Apparently this makes them irresistible, though they're doing nothing for me. There are squashed mini hot dogs, crumbs of potato chips, and broken cookies all over the floor. There are small puddles of spilled soda I make a mental note to avoid skidding on. None of the boys are housebroken, apparently.

I've noticed the Other Cass making his way through a pack of mints by the entrance. A guy who stays minty fresh versus some grubby boy who hasn't noticed a flattened frankfurter underneath his shoe: tough choice. Of course, it's not my choice to make. I'm just saying.

Char and I are standing with some other girls from our class. We are a mixture of *nice* girls who have never gone very far with boys (even boys with weeping cold sores), *awkward-looking* girls who probably won't get very far until the boys in question are much older and less superficial, and *serious* girls who haven't yet noticed that being this age is all about who likes who and who's been to which base. We are the observers. We could write an essay on what it looked like was going on the morning after, but no one will bother asking us because we're just that far removed from the real gossip. If I sound sorry for us, I'm not—in our school you're either nice or slutty, unless you're really beautiful, in which case you get to be in a whole different category. And I want the whole true falling-in-love thing, anyway, not some nasty tongue down my throat during Spin the Bottle.

"So who else is singing tonight?" Char asks. My dad showed me the list of students who'd signed up, demanding a detailed description of each person: looks, popularity, voice. I hyped them all just to see how nervous I could make him. Anxiety makes me sarcastic. So now he thinks I'm up against a range of musical geniuses who look like supermodels and have more followers than Kim Kardashian on Twitter.

I point out each of the Karaoke Kidz to Char, with the name of the artist they're singing.

"Justin Timberlake, Katy Perry, Coldplay, Rihanna, Beyoncé, Kings of Leon, old school Bon Jovi, Lady Antebellum. And me."

I feel a sudden wave of panic sweep up my chest, grab something in my throat, and pull it back down to my knees.

"Oh, God, I feel sick."

"Just get it over with," says Char. "Can't be *that* bad." Her mood hasn't improved, so much for caramel sympathy sauce. I wish Izzy would get here. At least I don't expect sympathy from her, and she has her own long-established brand of telling me to pull myself together.

"*You* feel like standing up there and singing?" I say. I keep it light but I'm getting really fed up with her.

"*I* wouldn't do anything I didn't want to do." (Says the girl who spends half her life in her room listening to Bieber because her dad's grounded her.) "Maybe you secretly love it," she says.

"This is my worst nightmare! What are you talking about?" She SHRUGS. Stop *doing* that, people!

"I just think that if you didn't want to do it on some level, you wouldn't. You'd say no." She looks around the room and won't look me in the eye.

It's not true. It's so frustratingly not true I don't know what to do with myself, but I have to get away from her. A line of girls desperate for the bathroom (or rather, the mirror in the bathroom) snakes down one side of the hall, so I can't go in there. There are no other groups I can join invisibly. Even if I lurked around the edges of one of them it would look like the equivalent of a warthog joining a pack of tigers, trying to blend in without getting its head bitten off. The Other Cass has deserted his post at the door, so I'd only have to sneak past Mrs. Roach to get some fresh air. I'm headed that way before I've had time to formulate a plan.

I'm tapping Mrs. Roach on the shoulder. Someone write me a script.

"Oh, hello, Kassidy. You excited? All set to go? Did you see Mr. Cowell walk in? No bodyguards or anything. Your dad said there'd be someone special here but I never imagined it would be—"

"Mrs. Roach, sorry, it's just that I heard someone . . . sniffing, in the bathroom."

"Sniffing? Well, I expect it's over some boy. It usually is, Kassidy."

"I don't think they were crying, Mrs. Roach." No idea where this came from, but by the backward scrape of her chair I'd say it was working.

"What *do* you think they were doing, then?"

"I really don't know anything about it, Mrs. Roach, but it sounded like they were . . . inhaling something, maybe?"

She's on her feet and headed for the girls' room before I've finished my sentence, but she rushes back to snatch the lockbox off the front desk and, bizarrely, her asthma inhaler.

"Keep an eye on things here," she says. Damn, now I feel guilty about deserting her post. But not that guilty.

There's a light rain and I know I shouldn't be out here, not least because Char spent ages straightening my hair, but the air cools my cheeks and finally I can take a deep breath, not restricted by the stress of tonight or the endless dry ice Dad insists on pumping onto the (empty) dance floor.

There's a crowd of popular kids about to walk up the path to the hall—fashionably late, of course, but not so fashionable that they could find anything better to do on a Friday night—so I decide to take cover around the side of the building in the space between the hall and the gym.

If I weren't so intent on walking straight in Char's boots I might have seen him earlier, but there he is, leaning against the wall with one foot up, his head down, taking a drag from a cigarette. I'm too far into the alleyway to back out now without seeming rude, or weird.

"Oh, hi," I say. "Sorry."

"Sorry? What for? Come in, quick, it's dry here." He points with his cigarette to a sheet of corrugated metal bridging the two buildings. "Want one?" He holds out the pack of cigarettes and my hand goes up instinctively, though I'm not sure what instinct it can be since I don't smoke.

"Actually, no thanks," I say. At that he toes his own into the ground, takes a small silver flask from the back pocket of his jeans, and takes a sip.

"Sshh, it's just vodka."

I watch him, fascinated. I'd never imagined him smoking or drinking. I haven't imagined him doing much, truth be told, except looking at me and talking to me on a computer and walking me to his little yellow car. Or sometimes banana.

"I guess you don't drink," he says. He doesn't make it sound like an accusation, just an observation.

"I drink," I say, and hit the ground with my heel a few times because I'm wincing at how hard I'm trying not to make it sound like a big deal. "I had some vodka before I came out."

"Well, feel free," he says. Now I'll have to. Oh, well: more courage.

The spout is so narrow I can't gulp it down like normal, and it burns my lips, but I take a good mouthful so I don't seem ungrateful for it.

"Thanks," I say. He puts the flask back and takes out a roll of mints.

"One of these now?" He takes one for himself and then so do I. We laugh as I struggle to get it out.

"Thanks." I pop it in and lean against the opposite wall, but my feet shuffle around for the perfect spot and I wish I was wearing my own shoes; it's definitely the boots.

"Nervous?" he says.

"Mm, a little," I try to reply without the mint falling out of my mouth.

"Must be even harder to do when your heart isn't really in it."

Oh, no, I don't want him to start talking about my dad. I couldn't bear it face-to-face.

"Um, my heart is in it. I'm fine—looking forward to it!"

"OK, then." He sounds like he doesn't believe me for a second but realizes I don't want to get all heavy. Is he perfect or what?

"What about your friend, Char—is she singing?"

My heart drops a bit when he asks about her, even though I know I should be happy. And maybe if she weren't being such a bitch it would be easier. Except it's probably me who's making her like that.

"No, she's not really into that sort of thing. She'll probably be a doctor or a lawyer or something. She's really smart."

He nods. Must be interested, so I keep going, but first I crunch my mint really quickly because I sound like I have a speech impediment. I'm sure I'll feel good about talking Char up in the end, though a tiny, tiny part of me . . . *no, forget it.*

"She's really nice, too. And *so* funny." Am I overdoing it?

"Right." He stops leaning against the wall. He seems taller than I remember. Or he's just closer. I'm too shy to look at him so I talk to my boots; Char's boots, I mean. Then his boots come into view. My heartbeat would rival a hummingbird's.

"She looks amazing tonight, don't you think?" My voice falters. I think he's going to kiss me. Shit. What do I do? I bring my hand to my mouth and cough, and leave my hand there — he can't kiss me if my hand is in the way. OK, keep talking about Char, eyes down. "*Such* a good figure, and she doesn't even know it. I think that makes her look even better, you know? Because she doesn't know it, not like some people who are just so self-aware and—"

He gently moves my hand, and I look at him, and he smiles a *You and I Both Know What I'm Going to Do* smile. My mouth is so dry I lick my lips accidentally, and then worry about what a come-on lip licking is.

Our noses are almost touching. I smell mint and then cigarette and I am giddy with nerves.

"Oh, Cass, I don't think we should. . . ." Even I don't believe myself. And then my eyes close and his lips press mine and his mouth is so warm I almost make a sound, but I don't, I just kiss him back and let myself melt.

I have absolutely no sense of time as the kiss goes on, and on, though my hands hover together near my chest not knowing

145

what to do, and it's only when I feel his hand move from the small of my back around my waist that I remember Char. Suddenly we are not a boy and a girl kissing, we are a boy and a bad friend; I am not one half of a movie kiss, I am disloyal and mean, and I can't do it anymore.

I squirm away a little and say:

"Sorry, I can't."

He gives me the same smile as if I'd said something cute and comes toward me again. It's more scary than romantic this time—I'm out of my depth. I put my hands on his chest to keep a distance between us, only this time he kisses me harder and presses me into the wall with his whole body and all I can think about is this tiny hard fragment of brick digging into my head. I push on his chest but he kisses me harder so I turn my head to the side and say, "Sorry, no," but his mouth is all over my neck and it's going way too fast, I'm scared and he's pressing me harder into the wall as I'm trying to urge him away from me, and then suddenly his hand goes up my top and I shriek, "Stop!" and shove him hard.

"What the fuck?" he says, and what I see in his face is nothing like the boy I've been thinking about day and night; he is someone else, and I am someone else, and he gives me this look of disbelief and backs out of the alley. He turns and runs down the path and it feels like his hands are still on my skin. I'm frozen rigid in this moment, and the only sound is the rain.

Chapter Thirteen

No One Else Will Do

The doorway glows red, orange, green, and Mrs. Roach is tapping her inhaler on the desk to the beat of the music coming from inside.

My senses are alive. There's the light rain on my face, the sound of tapping and of my breathing, and the sight of the moisture of my breath, and something new and awkward about me. The skin underneath my top heats up as if the feel of his hands will never go away, and I know that any minute I could cry, but that if I do, things will start to happen; people will come over and ask me why I'm crying and then I'll have to tell them. I don't think I can. What would I say?

I can't go down the dark path now, the way he went, and I can't stay out here, so I walk toward the lights.

"There you are, Kassidy," says Mrs. Roach. "I couldn't find any . . . *what you said*, but I did find three girls smoking, so thank you for being so helpful."

"Sure," I say. Red, orange, green. There are people on the dance floor now, glowing red-orange-green.

"Are you all right, dear?"

I can't get enough air into my lungs and contemplate asking for a puff of Mrs. Roach's inhaler.

"Kassidy?"

I think I say "Sure" again, and walk toward the red, orange, green. I can't think straight. I'm here, I'm back there; it's now, it's five minutes ago, and I didn't just let that happen.

Everything is ruined. I feel like crawling out of my own skin and hiding in a corner, but I'm supposed to sing now. I'm after this boy, Justin Timberlake. Dad waves from behind one of the giant speakers and jabs his finger toward the desk that Tony Ferrari is sitting at. Tony's teeth glow red, orange, green. Suddenly Char is standing right in front of me and for a second she is covered in black spots because I've been staring at the lights so long, but I blink and they go away and it's just Char, normal Char, the friendly face I need.

"You slut," she says. Is she talking to me? Does she mean me? "Well?" She hates me. Char's eyes really hate me. I think if I try to speak it will come out wrong. I should tell her what just happened; why can't I tell her? No, Char, I am not; it's not what you think. I just shake my head and say, "*No.*"

"I saw you," she says. "In that alley with his hands up your top. You whore." Do I imagine that she says, "Just like your mother"? I must.

"And give me back my fucking boots," she says.

I look down.

"Give them back *now*."

I can't take them off here. Why is she saying this? I'm so confused. If she saw me, she must know I didn't want to. I was pushing him away. She must have *seen*. So why is she saying *this*?

"*Please*, Char. It wasn't like that." My voice is like a whisper.

She knocks me as she storms past and grabs Izzy, who has just arrived, and drags her toward the bathroom. Izzy looks back at me as they go inside but I can't see her face. I need her, but I don't deserve her—Char wins Izzy's shoulder tonight, and now I have to get out of here.

I start to walk back outside and as the song finishes I start to run, and I feel the pinch of Char's boots as they smack along the wet pathway toward the gate. It clangs behind me and I'm out on the street. I keep running as I take my cell phone from my back pocket and scroll down to Mom's number. I almost press the wrong button, but when I hit the right one I stop dead and listen to my breathing and the phone ringing and ringing and ringing and: "Kass?"

"Mom."

"What is it, Kass? You sound out of breath."

"Mom, I need you to pick me up. Please. Please come."

"Of course I will, sweetie. But where's Dad? Where are you, Kass?"

"I'm on Pine Street near St. Joseph's, outside . . . the supermarket. Please come."

"OK. I'm leaving now. What's happened, Kass?"

"PLEASE, MOM, JUST COME!"

"I am. See you soon."

When she hangs up, I breathe out hard and look up and down Pine Street. I think I am myself again. And it's OK, my mom is coming.

✳ *Chapter Fourteen* ✳

Warning: This Phone Call Will Burn Your Ears

How ironic, it's the kind of night I love: The roads look prettier shiny with rain, and the car headlights stretch and streak into eye-piercing, beautiful rays of light. The *thud-squeak-thud* of the windshield wipers is soothing, rhythmic.

Mom is letting me be quiet. For a moment I wonder if that's the reason I needed her so badly. There's a guilty twinge that if I could have chosen Izzy or Char to turn to, I would have, but now that I'm here it feels right. Anyone else would have shaken it out of me by now, and I would have fought it, but we all know how much fight I have in me. (Even I didn't know how little, till now.) When she leaned over to open the passenger door I said, "Please don't ask," and all her worry for me was there in her forehead but she nodded and patted the seat, and now she's driving and I feel calmer just watching her.

"Does Dad know you've left?" she says.

"No."

She takes out her cell and starts to write a text.

"Tell him I'm sorry," I say.

"Don't worry, Kass. He shouldn't keep doing this, anyway. We've got to get a grip on things." She thinks I'm upset because of the karaoke. Get a grip on things? That doesn't sound like my mom talking.

"I didn't run out because of Dad. It wasn't him."

I have to defend him even though I know I'm dangling bait. She keeps her eyes on the road. Maybe she's the one who's baiting me.

"Are you OK?" she says. And I know she means, *Do I need to do anything drastic here or can I take your lead?*

"Yes. I'm OK. I just wanted you to come."

She changes gear and touches my leg briefly, eyes always ahead. I'm seeing her differently tonight. Her quietness isn't weak; it's strong. She seems gentle, not pointless. I am wrong about people; that's something I didn't know about myself before. And as for how wrong I was about me—I have that bottomless feeling you get when you're little and find out that something special isn't real: Santa Claus, the Tooth Fairy, or the idea of your parents being perfect.

"Can we get a coffee from Starbucks?" I say.

"Sure," she says, and pulls over. "You feel like something sweet? Latte with a shot of caramel or something?"

That is exactly what I feel like.

"Here, put some music on while you're waiting for me." Mom urges in a CD with a perfectly manicured finger. I wait till she's gone before switching it off. I'd rather listen to the rain than to Mariah Scary, but it makes me smile, and I know for sure I was right to call Mom.

We park just in front of our house and I feel like I haven't been here for ages. Was it really only this morning? I'm nervous about going inside but I want to, I just don't want it to be an invitation for questions about Tonight. I'm calling it Tonight in my head—a heavy but totally nonspecific label that will become Last Night and then That Night, I imagine, because I don't think it will ever really go away. The coffee at the bottom of the cup is ultrasweet but it's warming my hands so I don't want to let it go.

When we get to the front door Mom says, "Oh, I forgot, Maria will be here."

My eyes fill up and I look down at the coffee lid. But I can't cry yet. Maria is really nice, but I just want Mom to myself.

"I'm sorry, honey. She came over to babysit Raff. I'll get rid of her."

"How will you?" I say. Mom is too polite at the best of times.

"I will." The way she says it makes me believe in her instantly.

We walk in and I can tell by Maria's face that Mom must be giving her the kind of look that's, like, a secret code between best friends. But in her voice she gives nothing away.

"Hi, we're home."

"Hello, you're back early," she says, unsure. I just look all around the place like I've never seen it before. "Everything all right?" Maria stands awkwardly by the sofa, groping for her bag without taking her eyes off Mom, as if she's been told not to make any sudden moves.

"Actually, Kass has a terrible migraine. I'm going to take her upstairs, so . . ."

"I'll go, then. Feel better, Kass. Bye-bye now." Maria takes her coat and kisses Mom on the cheek and gives her a meaningful look. It's all very awkward but at least she's leaving. Mom steps outside with her for a second and lets a thin strip of cold air into our otherwise toasty house.

I'm still cupping the too sweet coffee as I sit on the sofa. I can see myself reflected in the television. Seems like it's someone else; maybe it's just because these are not my clothes. I want to go upstairs and change them but I can't quite get myself to move at normal speed.

Mom blocks my reflection by sitting on the coffee table in front of me; takes the coffee cup, takes my hands, leans forward.

"What is it, Kass?"

"Umm . . ." My chin twitches and my mouth turns down at the corners. I feel like a little girl.

"Nothing," I say.

Her eyes are already full of sadness.

"*Nothing*," I say again, but my voice and the word don't get along.

She grabs my arms and looks intense.

"Kass, please."

"I'm OK," I say, trying to wriggle free, annoyed by the sudden demand when I had almost believed she'd let Tonight go. "It wasn't . . . it was just . . . it wasn't . . . *I'm fine, get off, you're hurting me!*" I shout at her much too loud; I am not really shouting at *her*, am I? There's just no way I can tell her.

She deflates, she looks so sad and defeated; I feel awful for making her sad. Then she leans forward more, but it's too close, and now I can't look at her so I look down, but I can't look at Char's boots, either, so I look up and focus on the lamp shade.

She just about manages to say, "Tell me." It's like a whisper, like she has to know but can't bear it. "Is it about a boy?"

"*No!*" I start to cry but it's a sort of moan and I hide my head in a sofa cushion. Mom comes next to me on the sofa and holds me.

"Oh, Mom, I'm so stupid."

"You're not stupid, Kass." She says it like she's telling me off, but meanwhile she keeps holding me and I just let the sadness jerk my body inside her grip. I cry until there's nothing left, and after a few breaths I am calm, and I feel safe here with Mom. I feel safe, and sad, and stupid, and worn out.

Mom wipes the back of my hand with a tissue. Then she wipes my face.

"Thank you," I say. She puts her hands over my knees.

"Did someone hurt you?" It's only when she speaks that I realize she has been crying, too. There's an edge to her voice now.

"Mom, I really don't want to talk about it. Please. It's nothing that bad, really, please believe me, please."

I can see she wants to, but: "You have to understand, I'm your mother." She stands up and paces around and sounds pissed off. And that makes *me* pissed off because yes, she's *my mother*, and yet she's been letting my father dictate my entire life for years without stepping in and doing this sudden fierce act she's got going on now. She's *my mother* and yet she's usually so vacant we resort to snapping our fingers in front of her eyes. She's *my mother* and yet she pets and pampers Raff in a way I can never remember her doing for me. This has all gone wrong.

"And whatever this was, it happened at the disco?" she says, like I'm the chief suspect instead of the victim.

"No. Look, I'm not talking about it. It wasn't anything; not what you think. I'm fine, really. I just got a bit scared."

"You don't look fine. And where was Dad, for God's sake? What's going on here, Kassidy?"

Her anger starts me off again and I sob: "Nothing! Please shut up about it." How is this snowballing? Why does everything feel so horrible?

"I can't shut up about it. What happened?"

"Nothing!"

"Did you tell anyone else? Did anyone see you?"

"Only Char."

"And did you tell her? Why didn't she stay with you?"

I fall into the cushion again.

"Oh, God, I've ruined everything."

"No, no, Kass." We are both crying, both soft where before we were hard and angry, but now what is going through my head is what Char said about Mom. *Whore*. It's the last thing I can imagine anyone thinking about her. She's newborn bunny-wabbit innocent; I'm pretty sure Raff and I were both conceived immaculately (definitely in the dark, anyway). Mom turns me around and holds my head really tight to her chest. I don't want to tell her what Char said.

My hair is stuck to my face so I pull away from Mom and push my hair back and give out big puffs of air and lightly touch my eyelids because I can feel how swollen they are. Mom looks helpless without me near her, as if she needs to be holding me. She gets up and paces, dragging her hands through her hair and wiping them over her face. I've never seen her like this.

"Will you ever tell me?" she says. I don't answer. "This is very hard for me, Kass."

"I know, Mom. I'm sorry."

"Oh, sweetheart, what could you be sorry for?" she says, sitting down again and holding my hands.

There isn't just one answer, so I give none.

"I'm going to my room for a while," I say, and I let go of her hands. I can hear her weeping quietly as I climb the stairs.

Everything is different now. This room: The sounds aren't soothing, the sloping walls seem lower. The last time I was here, I was different. His hands are still there and the tiny fragment of brick still presses into the back of my head. Will I always feel like this? No one has ever touched me before. I imagined it happening, a lot—even with him—but never like that. I tried to stop him, didn't I?

Mom is different, too. I've never seen her go through such a range of emotions so quickly. I've never seen her angry. I've never seen her that upset, over me. Over Raff, maybe.

Raff. I'd forgotten about him. Did that bat-eared pipsqueak hear us? I go back downstairs to the landing. Mom and Dad's bedroom door is wide open and the bed is perfectly made, as it always is (except for when Dad is low, when the bed is hardly made at all). Raff's door is closed. I try the handle. Locked. I knock. Nothing.

"Raff?" I put my lips right up to the frame. I have no idea what I'd say to him if he answered, but I need to know if he heard us.

Nothing.

I'm about to go down the next flight of stairs to figure out with Mom how to handle Dad, when I hear her talking to someone.

"She's upstairs . . . I don't know, she seems very upset. I just don't know." Her voice undulates: waves of quiet sadness and rage. "She doesn't want to tell me—I can't make her, can I?"

It must be Dad on the phone, and he will try to make me tell. I will never, ever tell him.

"I know, darling," says Mom. I don't think I've ever heard her call him that. They don't have names for each other, just their real ones.

"I don't know, but I've got to deal with things with Paul, get him to see someone, stop all this from going on and on. . . ."

Paul? My dad, Paul? Then who's she talking to?

". . . yes, I'll call you . . . soon. Oh, Graham, don't talk to Charlotte about this. Please. I think they've had a falling out. . . ."

Graham? What? *Graham?* Charlotte? Falling out . . . oh, my . . .

"I don't know," Mom hisses, like she's trying to shout quietly. "I can't think about that right now. I've got to be here for Kass. I'll call. Bye . . . yes, sorry, love you, too. Bye."

✳ *Chapter Fifteen* ✳

I Guess Her Face Was So Pretty, She Thought She'd Get Another One (and Other Bad Jokes to Make About Your Mom Being Unfaithful)

"Mom."

I've walked to the foot of the stairs silently, and I stand there and feel my socks smoosh into the carpet as I sway very slightly, back and forth, until I take hold of the banister. Mom spins around and holds the phone away from her as if it's one of Dad's socks.

"Oh. Kass."

"Was that Dad?" I say.

"That? No." Her cheeks are turning from Perfectly Pale through all the shades to Uncomfortably Pink. (If I don't mock her inwardly, God knows what I'll do to her outwardly.)

"Oh. Who was it, then?" I am praying so hard that she won't answer. I need her to lie to me so that I can get out of here— I have to go back upstairs and *take this in*. But right now I am on autopilot.

"It was Maria. I just had to . . . well, she was obviously worried after seeing us come in like that, and—oh, Kass, I'm *sorry*." Her face does that crumpling thing again, only this time I don't feel bad for her. "I just had to talk to someone." She looks helpless. Forlorn. Like always. Only she is not helpless, she is a liar.

"What did Maria say?" I can feel my voice giving way to my emotions, but it doesn't matter because she will just think I am upset about what she already knows I am upset about. We are both liars, then. *Just like your mother*, Char said. Char, my former best friend who is now not my best friend because my mother is a . . . No, I can't believe this. But there she is, scratching her head and frowning, thinking of the next lie.

"Well, she thought . . . she thought I should leave you alone for a while."

"Really? Is that what Maria said?" When I say the *M* of *Maria* my lips quiver together, betraying the tears that could come any minute, but Mom isn't really looking or listening attentively; she's twitchy, distracted. She just nods. Then she sidesteps to the coffee table and puts the phone down as if it's a loaded gun. I can see she's too scared to come near me. Maybe her aura knows that my aura is like an electric fence right now.

"I want you to stop mentioning it now," I say.

"OK. I'll stop."

"So you haven't called Dad, then?"

"I texted him to say you were safe with me," she says. "He'd left so many messages on my cell phone. I was just about to call him."

"But you called Maria first? Dad will be frantic!"

161

"Well, yes. It was just . . . I didn't know what you'd want me to tell Dad, for a start." She looks as if she's miming a rigorous hand-washing ritual, and the nervous throat clearing has begun.

I could tell her that I don't even want to look at her, here and now, but I can't stop myself from pressing buttons. She called Char's dad before she called mine. She called Graham Roebuck—tyrant, bully, music-censoring cold fish and everything else that Izzy and I have called him over the years— before she called her own husband, my dad.

"I don't want you to tell Dad *anything*," I say. It's so hard to say these words, instead of the accusations I want to make, that my throat is starting to ache, the way it does when Dad makes me sing the same song over and over. "I mean it, Mother." Now it's my face crumpling up—all it took was the thought of the look on his face if he knew what she'd been up to—and I have to put my hand out to stop her coming closer. "No." I breathe in deeply so I can speak again for a moment. My temples are pulsing with the pressure—there is Mom's secret, and mine, and they will both kill Dad. "I really, really need this to be our secret, Mom. Don't tell him. Say I ran out because I was too stressed to go through with the song. He'll believe that."

"But, Kass, I don't even know what *did* happen—"

"*Mom.* It's something for me to deal with. I'm just asking you to keep one secret for me. So please, *please, will you?*" I am practically bursting as I say this.

"OK, calm down, I will."

Of course she will; she knows all about secrets.

"And Raff, too. He's not answering his door. You don't think he heard us, do you?"

"No, darling, he'll be asleep, I expect. Maria said he'd gone up to bed with a sore tummy. I'll check on him later."

Darling? But I thought that grand title belonged to Graham. Charlotte's dad: the Remote Control. Everything that's coming out of her mouth is making me feel sick. How long has she been lying? For the first time in my life I notice the lines on her face. Her mascara has run. Her hair is out of place. She no longer resembles a store mannequin.

"Can I get anything for you?" she says.

I don't want to tell her that I'm hungry. It feels like I shouldn't be, after Tonight and now This. What's the matter with me? I think back to the Christmas fruitcake I scarfed down in Char's bathroom, then the feel of Char's house creeps up my spine; the closed doors and the strange stillness. Now I picture Mom and Graham behind the doors. Were their ears pressed up against them, listening for our footsteps? Did they smile at each other when they heard me go by?

"Nothing," I say, the word jamming in my windpipe. "I don't want anything."

She looks at the phone and says, "I should call Dad now. Don't worry, I'll tell him all this is about the singing. Maybe he'll even forget about the whole *X Factor* thing now, leave you in peace."

She says it as though I'd be lucky for that to happen; as if I'm *lucky*.

"I don't want him to leave me in peace." My throat is in agony,

163

like I can barely get the words out, like I can't put enough meaning into them.

"But you hate all that stuff he puts you through. Don't look at me like that." She almost adds *please*. So polite, so soft, such *grace*; so cold, butter wouldn't melt in her mouth.

"What would you know? What, after all these years, suddenly you're going to help me out? Well, don't bother. I'm going back to my room. *Don't* let Dad come up when he gets home."

"I'll do my best."

"Mom. Do whatever you have to do." I stare at her so hard. Can she guess what I'm thinking? She looks guilty enough. I hate her and her lies, and it's all so messed up in my head.

When I get to my room I'm more out of breath than the stairs would have made me; it's all sinking in. The times she's worked late—worked late, or been with *him*? She's been coming home, cooking for us, lovingly preparing spaghetti carbonara and a big fat lie for dessert; she's swallowed us saying "Thanks, Mom!" and out she's gone with a spring in her step from the new black shoes she must have bought to impress *him*. How *could* she, with that toad of a man? I feel so stupid; I feel the way you do when someone at school pulls your chair out as you're about to sit down.

From my desk I pick up a photo in a frame that says *Best Friends*: me, Izzy, and Char. It's mostly me and Izzy because Char's camera-shy, but she looks so sweet and she's looking at me like she thinks I'm something special—not the girl who stole the boy she loves, and not the girl whose mother stole her dad. We're all smiling—stupid, smiling girls who have no idea that my mother is about to ruin our lives.

I backtrack; I feel like I'm watching a home movie of my life when I picture Char getting on the bus, that first morning she didn't seem herself. That was almost three weeks ago—she's been carrying this around all that time. Why didn't she *tell* me? How did she keep something like this in? I can't ask her; I can't ask any of the million questions because I've ruined things between us. She was right—I'm just like my mother.

I put the photo facedown on the desk and flick off the light, and flick it back on when the darkness takes me back to the alley. Toe to heel I ease the boots off, leaning against the wall, and put them neatly together in a corner by the dusty cello. I sit on my bed, close my eyes, and tilt my head back. I hold my breath for Dad's return, as if from up here I'd be able to hear anything but the wind skating over the skylight or the pigeons' babble. Instead I imagine what Dad might be saying to Mom on the phone, and her replies:

— *I've been worried sick, Grace. What the hell is going on?*
— *Calm down—*
— *Don't tell me to calm down, just tell me what happened.*
— *It's . . . nothing, it was just that she didn't want to go through with it. The song.*
— *She's never done that to me before. Not since . . . I don't believe it. She wouldn't run out on me like that.*

165

– Well, she did.
– Yes, but why, Grace, WHY?
– I don't know.

I turn over and press my face into my hands and cry noise-lessly. I have betrayed my best friend, and myself, and I can never erase what's happened. Tonight I have fallen apart and I have no one, *no one* to turn to.

✳ *Chapter Sixteen* ✳

Oh, Brother

I don't feel as if I've been asleep, and yet the scratching noise seems like it's been going on for a while and I'm only just noticing it. Then there's a sound like a hiss. I'm on my back in the dark and the moon through the skylight looks like smudged chalk. *Scratch. Hiss.* I become aware of my fingertips and my legs and my eyelids, swollen and sore as I blink.

"Kassss," comes a whisper. The hiss is my name.

Scritch-scratch on the door. It's Raff.

I get up and open the door before I've had time to decide whether or not I want to.

"Can I talk to you?" he says.

"About what?" Behind him the staircase is dark, and there isn't a trace of glow coming from downstairs. This usually means that Dad has locked up and gone to sleep. Can that really be? Did Mom fend him off, and if so, how? I'm so angry with myself for falling asleep.

"I need to come in."

"Raff, I'm not in the mood."

"Yeah, I know, but—"

"*What* do you know? Did you hear me and Mom?"

"I swear I didn't. What, about the karaoke?"

"No, not that."

"I don't know anything." It's weird, he seems genuine. Everyone is different tonight. "I didn't come up to talk about you, believe it or not."

I can't quite put my finger on his tone, but I feel instantly guilty. Suddenly I see a thirteen-year-old boy instead of the Enemy.

"OK. Come in." I switch on my desk lamp and sit on the chair. Raff is short enough to stand up straight in my room, and he chooses to do that rather than sit on the futon. "What is it?"

He blows out a huge sigh and runs his hands through his hair and over his face, as though he's doing an impression of some really stressed-out executive who's just lost a million.

"I need your help," he says, raising his arms and then letting them flop against his sides as if in surrender to the worst possible scenario he could have imagined.

"I don't have any money, Raff."

"I know."

Now I'm really curious; I didn't think Raff could even pass a bowel movement without it being money related. He's still doing the stressed-out executive thing, wiping his face with his hands as if he's trying to clean something off.

"Raff, I'm tired and I really don't need your shit now. Either tell me and get it over with or just leave me alone." I know what I'm saying is harsh even as it's coming out, and I haven't got the strength for one of our usual fights, anyway, so I say it softly and in a monotone.

"I will," he says. He puts both hands in his pockets and talks to his ridiculous reindeer slippers. "I'm in a bit of trouble—"

"Oh, great, what have you done now?" I seem to have split out of my calm countenance. It's the Raff Factor.

He glares at me for interrupting and even I agree that it was annoying of me, so I mime lip-zipping.

"I haven't *done* anything. But me and Luke got talking to this gang and they want us to join."

"You *what*? Why? To do what?"

"Wait, I'm getting to that part! Just shut up and listen for once."

That told me. It really did, actually—it's like I can't help picking away even though I can see this is hard for him.

"They want us to be lookouts on a few jobs."

"*Jobs?* What, *crime*, you mean?"

"Yes, Kass, crime. Jesus, only small stuff. A few cars."

"Cars? Doing what to cars?"

"Well, taking them." He looks at me as if I'm the last person on the planet to try carjacking.

"Huh," I say. I'm gradually swallowing all of this. I thought he just sold our stuff on eBay and used Mom's credit card. This is like some horrible flash of what being a parent is like. I am *never* having kids.

"But I don't want to. I mean, they're all right but they've done some heavy-duty stuff that I just don't wanna get into."

"Oh, God, like what?"

"Doesn't matter. Just, one time, they really hurt this kid who was gonna be a witness in court against them, and he nearly died."

"Oh, my God, RAFF!"

"What? All right, calm down, *I* didn't do it!"

"It doesn't matter, why are you even talking to these people?"

"I knew you wouldn't understand." He grimaces, then flops onto the futon and puts his head between his hands.

"What is there to understand? Just don't do it, don't get involved. End of story."

"It's not that easy. Luke wants us to do it. He says if I don't he'll tell the gang I'm gonna go to the police."

"But why would he do that? He's your friend."

"Yeah, well, we had a big argument about it and he said he's sick of me making all the decisions and now he wants to be part of this gang." He looks all hot and his fingernails are dirty—I feel so sorry for him. I wish I could hug him. But then right out of my sympathy comes this anger and before I know it I'm shouting at him again:

"Well, what the hell am I supposed to do about it? You idiot, you deserve everything you get!"

"Shut up, Kass, just shut up!" he cries, and looks up at me with his tearstained, grimy, hot little face.

We freeze at the sound of Mom's muffled voice coming from downstairs:

"What's going on up there?"

I open the door and shout, "NOTHING!" and slam it again. The contents of my stomach have turned sour. With me silent, Raff resumes talking.

"I need you to fix it, Kass."

"Sure, I'll just grab my AK-47 and deal with them for you."

"Kass."

"Sorry."

"Do you even know what kind of gun that is?"

"A big one?"

He smirks, almost in sympathy, it seems. One look at his grubby face and suddenly I am filled with the kind of love I know I used to feel for him, when life wasn't so complicated. I feel like I should have stopped all this from happening—how could I have let my little brother slip out of our world and into this mess?

"I thought of a plan," he says, calming down.

"Me, too. It's called telling Mom and Dad."

Raff looks at me as if I just suggested he put on a dress and do the Hokey Pokey.

"NO. That's the last thing I can do. That will make things a thousand times worse, believe me." I know he's right: We can't tell Mom and Dad. We need to talk damage control, and that means keeping this stress as far away from Dad as possible, especially now that my lying mother may have put this whole family in jeopardy.

I start to tug clumps of hair from the nape of my neck and focus on Raff.

"The only person who can stop Luke is his brother," he says. I'm struck dumb. "Hello, Kass? Are you listening?"

"Go on."

"I need you to call him. Say you overheard me and Luke talking, and explain the whole thing. Say Luke's supposed to meet them on Saturday to agree to do the job. Fourth level of the shopping center parking garage. Cass is the only one who can stop him. Luke worships him, 'cause they don't have a dad and stuff. Cass does everything for him . . . OK? Will you do that?"

My voice comes out stuttering.

"Why can't you? You do it; why, why can't you? Why me?"

"I don't want Luke to know I've told you. It'll sound better if you say you heard us. He knows you're always listening at my door."

"I am not!"

Raff laughs, but I feel like I'm going to explode with how awful this situation is.

"Chill out. Can you do it? Please. You're my big sister." Great. He played the Big Sister Card. There's almost nothing higher. "Anyway, you and Cass are kind of cozy, aren't you? He told Luke he likes you. Good, right?"

He likes me. He likes me so much he pushed me up against a wall. I didn't think I could feel worse, but I do now. There's no way I can tell Raff why I don't want to make that phone call.

"How did you even end up in this mess, Raff? How?"

"You don't know what it's like to be me in this family. Dad doesn't even know I'm there half the time. You're his little angel and I might as well not exist. It doesn't matter which of his moods he's in."

"Look, I might have Dad on my back all the time but you've got Mom to take care of you. You've always been her favorite."

"Maybe," he says, eyes down. "But she's been a bit busy lately."

He knows. Oh, God, Raff knows about Mom and Char's dad.

"You know something?" I say. He sits up.

"Maybe. Do you?"

"Maybe. Yes. Found out tonight."

"Shit. Do you know who it is?"

"Yes."

"Shit."

That's all we can say about it. It's so unbelievable and so awful that there aren't any useful words we can swap. I can't bear to think of him weighed down with all of this. He hasn't seemed different at all, so it must be churning him up inside, curdling what little innocence he has left. He might know more than me about gangs and stealing, but what can he know about relationships and affairs and what it means for our mother to betray us all like that? I have to be the brave one; I have to let him be thirteen again.

We are quiet for a long time, and then I say, "I'll do it. I'll make the call."

He exhales heavily, as if he'd been holding his breath for my answer.

"Great," he says. And hands me a piece of paper with a number scrawled in black ink. "You've just gotta do it by next Saturday."

✳ Chapter Seventeen ✳

Spotless Kitchen, Dirty Liar

I come downstairs the next morning, and for a second I think I'm in that really annoying movie about the guy who has the same day over and over again. My dad smiles at me from the kitchen doorway as he wipes his hands with a dishcloth. This smile says, *I'm going to pretend last night didn't happen, just to freak you out.* Mom smiles at me from the front door, where she is opening the mail. This smile says, *I'm guilty as sin but I can fool my daughter, easy as pie.*

I can't look at her for long; I have to pretend she's not there until I've figured out what's going on and how we can stop Dad from finding out. He couldn't cope. This could push him permanently over the edge.

Raff briefly looks in my direction from his position in front of the television, Xbox control in his lap. This look says absolutely nothing I can figure out, except maybe, *Oh, it's you.* The tenderness I felt before I fell asleep with my scared little brother next to me evaporates, and I make for the kitchen to distract myself with breakfast.

Dad hovers behind me with his dishcloth, pretending to have something more to do in our pristine kitchen. I'd suggest that the bananas need a polish, but I don't want to talk. At least I can be sure that he doesn't know what really happened last night. He looks like he doesn't have a care in the world, but he must be bursting to ask me why I ran out on the karaoke. Let him simmer; it's for his own good.

I think the toaster's broken — I'm sure the bread has been in there a good half hour with no sign of popping up. Dad puts jars in front of me — suggestions for what to put on my toast: peanut butter, marmalade, honey, and there's also a jar of stuffed green olives for some reason. The man's a liability.

"So, a week to go," he says. When I glance around he's rubbing a spot on the vinyl tablecloth with a dishcloth-covered finger. I try to remain calm and focus on the thin orange bars glowing in the toaster.

"Wasn't that Tony guy good?" he says. I say nothing.

"Take the day off today, Kassidy. You deserve it." Why do I?

"I know I've been pushing you hard. Maybe too hard. But it's only because I know deep down you want this. Right? Right, Kassidy?" He's looking at me like a child who's just overheard some awful truth in the playground and needs some reassurance so he can go back to the Land of Make-Believe. How can I be the one to pop the bubble?

"It was my voice. I must have strained it. I knew I couldn't perform and I freaked out. Sorry, Dad." I sound unconvincing at best, but his smile widens and he waves his dishcloth like a victory flag.

"I knew that's what it'd be. We'll go all out with our rehearsals beginning tomorrow, but let's really up your intake of salt water. We can't take chances. I've got a new relaxation CD for you, and we'll do those breathing exercises, and . . ."

As he keeps on talking I lean toward the toaster and my eyebrows start to heat up. Now my eyeballs feel hot, and the countertop is digging into my stomach, and the combination of those sensations makes Dad's voice seem very far away.

"Sure, Dad," I say, and the toast pops up just as Mom walks in.

"Everything OK in here?" she says. "Kass?"

"Everything's fine!" says Dad, and he plants a firm kiss on Mom's cheek as he leaves with a spring in his step.

"Kass?" says Mom.

"Like Dad said. Fine."

I eat the toast in my bedroom, thinking and chewing and only half aware of the radio in the background. The volume is set to 3—it needs to be on number 4 to hear the actual words being spoken by the DJ, but I have no desire to turn it up. I just don't want it to be *too* quiet in here.

"Kass?" Something other than knuckles is knocking on my door.

"What is it, Mom? I said I was *fine*."

"Can I come in?"

Instead of answering I make faces at the door, but I want to know what she's making that noise with so I get up and open it.

"Here, it's Izzy for you," she says. So it was the phone. Well, what did I think it was going to be? Maybe a big sign saying *I'm a Dirty Liar*?

I mouth, *I'm not here, I'm not here*, and shoo the phone away from me. Mom tries to give it to me again, so I shut the door in her face. I hear her apologize to Izzy and promise I'll call back.

We stand on either side of the door. My breathing is heavy and my heart thumps with all the anger I feel toward Mom.

"Kass, can we talk?"

She sounds so calm and concerned, which makes me even angrier.

"No, thanks," I say.

"I'm worried about you."

Sure. That's why you're sleeping with — oh, God, I can't believe it; it will never seem real as long as I live — my best friend's dad.

"Don't bother," I say.

"I can't help it, I'm your mom."

Everything she says sounds cheap. I feel like ramming through the door and flattening her with it. I want to scream at her until my skull splits open with all the pressure that's been building up since I overheard that phone call. A few miles away my best friend has this stewing inside her, too. Except, because my mother handed down not her skinny legs or her perfect hair but her taste for betrayal, we can't even console each other.

"Just go," I say, spitting through my teeth. But when she does my rage deepens, and I move around my tiny bedroom like a caged animal, thinking of her picking me up last night when I needed someone I trusted more than life, and thinking of Raff with the weight of Mom's secret on his shoulders, and thinking of my poor, clueless dad with his pathetic dishcloth and his idiotic dreams and his cheating wife.

I have made up my mind. I will help my brother out of his mess, and I will go to one final audition for my dad, and I will never, ever forgive my mom.

It's just after midnight; I've been trying so hard to fall asleep that I'm almost groaning with the exertion. I throw off the covers as if it's all their fault and leave the room in disgust. I have absolutely no idea where I'm going, or what I'll do when I get there, but as I walk down the stairs the house is so eerily still that I get the urge to do something sneaky.

The hum of the fridge goes up an octave as if to let me know that it sees me here—that it has clocked me eyeing Mom's handbag hanging on the kitchen door. I open the fridge, take out the orange juice, and have a swig from the bottle, just to let the fridge know who's boss. On my way out of the kitchen I casually unhook the bag's strap from the door handle and go to sit in Dad's armchair.

Mom's bag is as neat as ever. She uses each compartment diligently, and they contain useful things: a miniature sewing kit, a pack of hand wipes, a pack of normal tissues (that's two kinds of wipes; is she prepared or what?), sugar-free chewing gum, a black ballpoint pen, a red ballpoint pen, a small notepad (completely blank), the world's smallest umbrella, headache pills, indigestion pills, and a bizarre miniature tool kit with floral handles that looks like it was made for Barbie. All the items are clean, as if brand-new. In contrast, no item can exist in my bag for more than half a day without becoming smeared with lip gloss and then covered with teeny-weeny bits of nondescript bag dirt. Pens explode in my bag. Things go missing. My bag is like a cross between the Bermuda Triangle and the town dump.

I take out Mom's phone. When I say her phone is retro, I mean I need two hands to lift it. I go through her list of contacts; she has someone listed as "G." I feel sick. The number is a cell I haven't seen before.

She only has two texts in her inbox, which already seems weird. One is from Raff. Home at 5. Love ya Mom. That takes my breath away. I can't remember the last time I told Mom I love her. Anyway I don't now; I hate her.

The other message is from "G." Sat a.m., my place. Can't wait. x.

Oh, God. I throw the phone back in and hang the bag where it was before. This is a real live affair my mother is having. I knew that—I knew it before, but now there is real live proof, and a real live meeting taking place in a few days during which disgusting things will happen between my mother and that man. I feel like running up to my parents' bedroom and shaking my mother awake, screaming at her until all this pent-up anger is flushed out.

But I can't. I have to think of Dad. All around me is the smell of the dying flowers he bought her: just a faint hint of rose, now, overpowered by something putrid. Why can't anyone else smell it?

✳ Chapter Eighteen ✳

Can I Have My Lame Old Life Back Now, Please?

It's another Monday morning, and I'm standing in a very light rain, though I could easily take refuge under the bus shelter. I must be turning into some kind of hair masochist — deliberately causing major frizz as if that will ensure that no boy ever likes me again. Not that I needed any help in that department before.

On the surface everything looks the same, but nothing is. None of the important things, anyway, but even the stuff that's stayed put seems unreliable now. I hold tighter to the railing when I climb onto the bus, and check the seat for gum more thoroughly than normal. I don't do any of my usual thinking, either. I just look around, gradually taking in the objects and sounds that form my ordinary world.

"Hey, K," says Izzy. She's smiling but her eyes say, *Oh, Furbs, what* have *you done*? I remember now that I was supposed to call her back.

"It wasn't how she said it," I say, remembering Char stealing Izzy away on Friday night.

"You didn't kiss him?"

I blush.

"No. I mean, yes, I did but . . . I don't want to talk about it, actually."

Izzy grows even taller in her seat. I cross my arms and my knees clamp together; I angle them toward the window and huddle against it.

"Fine, we won't," she says. There are three stops left till Char gets on. If I had the slightest clue how I'm supposed to feel about her, I might be able to brace myself.

"What did you do this weekend, then?" says Izzy.

"Nothing."

"Oh, OK. So why didn't you call me back?"

"I just didn't. Sorry." I know I don't sound sorry but I'm not in the mood to be told off by another friend. She doesn't know what I've been through these past couple of days.

"I needed to talk to you," she says. "About my parents. They're . . . getting back together, and—"

"Ha! You're kidding!" I can tell by her expression that bursting out laughing is the least appropriate reaction I could have chosen. And, yes, I suppose it's not that funny that Izzy has just spent two years in therapy to get over her parents splitting up, or that every single day she has a new observation about why they were so wrong for each other, or that they actually compete—not just in front of Izzy but in front of her friends, too—to say the most offensive things about each other. It's not funny, but it is ridiculous.

I wipe the smile off my face; Izzy looks very grave.

"Come on, Izz, it's great if you think about it."

"I *am* thinking about it," she snaps.

"OK, sorry."

We have to pause it there because we're at Char's bus stop. Only there's a distinct lack of Char. I'm sort of relieved, but now I'm desperate to know why she's not coming to school—or not on the bus with us, anyway. I half listen as Izzy goes on about her loved-up parents, and I try to sort through the jumble of feelings in my head about our mutual friend. It feels like I'm rooting around in a black trash bag full of black clothes in a dark room trying to find something to wear.

Whatever she's said to me recently, I can't help feeling sorry for Char. Her personality may have turned from angel food cake to rat poison in the past week, but she's had a lot to deal with—that awful father (who is apparently irresistible to my stupid mother), and her mom leaving them (at least some-one's mother has taste), and finding out about this affair or whatever it is.

But then there's the guilt. Because it's my mom involved I feel responsible, not to mention skin-crawlingly embarrassed. But then there's the feeling of injustice. Char is so angry with me—she blames *me*! It's fine for me to blame myself—that's my decision—but it's so unfair for someone else to blame me.

Then there's the rage. Could this be the end of our friendship? This awful, embarrassing, unbelievable thing? And finally there's the awkwardness, because even if this could mean the end of our friendship, I don't think I can stick my neck out and save it.

So that's pity, guilt, injustice, rage, and awkwardness: sounds like a pretty healthy concoction. Nothing at all to worry about. And as soon as there's a massive sale at Carpets-R-Us I'll have something to brush it under.

I decide there and then not to tell Izzy the full extent of this emotional meltdown; I dread to think what she'd diagnose.

"Are you even listening to me?" she says. Oops. I really wasn't.

"Of course I am!"

"What did I just say, then?"

"Don't be like that, Izz." I feel bad for not explaining why I'm being so vacant this morning, but it's best locked up. I just know what Izzy would say. If I tell her about Cassian coming on so strong: "You owe it to womankind to see that justice is done." If I tell her about the trouble Raff's in: "It's the classic second-child syndrome." If I tell her about my mom and Char's dad: "Get it out in the open; you have to lance the boil." (Ugh. I prefer my boils unpopped, thanks.) And if I tell her my fears about Dad, she'll tell her mom, who knows all sorts of people who specialize in locking people away for their own good and putting their kids into the care of the state — they've told me enough horror stories.

So I'll keep quiet about it all for now. Izzy would understand if she knew.

I walk home the usual way, and I'm so caught up in my thoughts that I pay no attention to the rhythmical *stamp-stamp-stamp* until I see Stamping Man almost bent over double in between two parked cars, pounding his feet on the road. My heart skips and I walk in a curve to get farther away. His face is a blank. Why has he moved to this street? He's been stamping on the other route for as long as I can remember.

I walk faster, now in time to the stamping, now faster still. Even after I reach our street I can still hear him, though I can't be sure if it's a real sound or just my mind playing tricks. The more I try not to think about it, the louder the stamping seems. But what am I afraid of? The Stamping Man just stamps. And anyway, I'm home now.

Raff is sitting outside our place, eyes locked on his new BlackBerry—stolen, clearly, though he managed to convince Mom and Dad he'd won it in a raffle at school. He lifts his legs and drops them so his sneakers bounce off the wall. I throw an empty juice carton at his head to test the hypnotic power of the BlackBerry. He catches it with one hand without looking and throws it over his shoulder to land in the open garbage can.

"Idiot," he says. I can't argue.

"What are you doing out here?" I say.

"Forgot my keys."

"Oh. I'm surprised you didn't just call your crew to shimmy up the drainpipe and break in."

"Funny, Kass." He slips the BlackBerry inside his school

blazer and does me the courtesy of actually looking at me.

"What?" he says. Charming.

"Um, *nothing*," I say. And with that scintillating conversation in the bag we head for the front door.

We both stop dead in our tracks when we hear clattering coming from the kitchen, and then exhale tension like balloons with slow leaks when it becomes obvious that it's only Mom inside. She's usually home at least an hour after us.

Since Raff hinted that he knows about Mom and the Remote Control, I've been watching the way he is with her now. I can't see any difference. Either he doesn't *really* know, or he knows and this is just further proof that he is hollow inside. Or maybe he loves her so much that he has already forgiven her. I don't want to think about that possibility too much, because I have already decided that my relationship with her is completely over.

The clattering must have been all the vases — she's stuffing a black trash bag with the dead roses and pouring the rancid water down the sink. How can she do that and look so calm? I guess symbols are totally lost on her: symbols and morals.

"You're late, Raff," she says, all sugary. "You didn't have detention, did you?" Detention? Detained by the police is more likely.

"I was waiting outside. Forgot my key."

"Oh, silly." She tweaks his face. "Why didn't you just ring the doorbell?"

"You're not usually here," I say, not that she was talking to me. She looks over as if she's only just noticed I'm in the room, but then there's this fake smile.

"How was your day?" she says.

"Fine." I try on breezy for size, having finished with surly. "Char wasn't there, though."

"Oh?" says Mom. She's fishing for more but pretends she's not by sucking on a finger she's obviously just pricked on a rose thorn. And she *still* doesn't get the symbolism? Amazing.

"We figure Char's stupid dad has finally lost it and chained her up for good."

Mom stays quiet. Raff nudges me and mouths, *No.* I mouth something else. He mouths something else, and I don't think either of us knows what we're mouthing anymore, so he takes action.

"Mom, I really need help with my English homework," he says. "It's poetry."

My little psychological torture session is over, and so soon. I can't believe he's on her side.

"OK, sweetie, go and get changed and we'll look at it at the kitchen table while I make dinner."

Before Raff goes upstairs, and when he's sure Mom's out of earshot, he whispers to me:

"You're still gonna help me, aren't you?"

"Yes, I said I would."

"When are you gonna call him?"

"Soon."

"Thanks, Kass." His oversize bag smacks against his back as he runs up to his bedroom. Mom reaches around me from behind and squeezes me, and I twist out of her arms.

"How are you doing?" she says.

What I want to say to her is: *I'm pretty much the worst I've ever been.* I also want to say: *I always knew I had to hold up my end of the bargain by not giving Dad any extra stress—it was hard, but I could handle it. I thought it was what you wanted, too. But there you are, living some other life, and you don't have a clue what your children are going through.*

And just when I'd think I was done, I'd want to add: *What I really, really need right now is for my mom to chase away the monsters. But I'm on my own. I even have proof about what could happen to Dad now. The pamphlet says,* In other cases, the symptoms seem to come after a life crisis, stress, or illness. *A life crisis. Stress. What do you think you're doing, playing with our lives? You don't care about Dad. Or Raff. Or me.*

What I actually say is: "Tired."

It's easy enough to shrug her off.

✳ *Chapter Nineteen* ✳

Simon Says . . .

I'm in my room, with a dull ache in the back of my throat from singing arpeggios really badly (even Dad struggled to hide his wincing). On my desk there's another glass of salt water, which will no doubt go the same way as the last one (into the porcelain wishing well). After the singing, Dad wanted to "work on your personality, Kassidy. Simon says he's looking for an instant affinity with the audience."

"I hate crowds," I said.

"That's OK, you can be the enchanting wallflower who blossoms before our very eyes."

I knew it would be pointless to tell Dad that I had absolutely no intention (much less hope) of "blossoming" on national television. It still amazes me that he can't see I have *X Factor Blooper Reel* written all over me, but I'm trying to get the balance right between keeping Dad happy and maintaining some vague level of sanity in myself, which means carefully guarding my privacy.

"In that case, I'd better go upstairs so I can practice visualizing the ideal *X Factor* personality," I said.

"Would it help if I invited Tony over? He said he'd help out anytime. *For free*, Kassidy!"

Tony? Who the . . . ? Oh, *Tony Ferrari*, the Doppelganger from Hell.

"I'm better off with just some peace and quiet," I said.

"You got it." Thumbs-up from Dad, who then went shouting "PEACE AND QUIET FOR KASSIDY!" into the kitchen and living room, for the attention of all two other occupants of this house.

Anyway, I'm up here now, safe in my turret with pigeon surround sound, but I feel so feeble and stressed out that the most I can bring myself to do is sit slightly comatose in front of my computer, drifting deeper and deeper inside the World Wide Web as I click on link after link.

I Google *Tony Ferrari* and find his website, which is bad on so many levels. Then I Google *tonsillitis* because Izzy texted me earlier to tell me that Char had it and wouldn't be around for a while and that I should get in touch. Maybe I should send her a two-in-one card: *Get Well Soon, and Sorry My Mom Is Sleeping With Your Dad*. I Google myself to see if any interesting Kassidy Kennedys have emerged recently, but all I find are the Kassidy Kennedys I've Googled before, who belong to the Pony Club or enjoy running cross-country, neither of which I can identify with on any level, being someone who is scared of all animals with teeth as well as someone who dislikes breaking into a sweat/wearing shorts.

I've been staring so hard my pupils are starting to ache when:

stix: hi?

All these things happen at once: my heart stops my left hand goes to my chest my right hand presses the button on the monitor and it fizzes to black.

I just stare at the screen. Everything that happened comes back to me, only faster and with parts missing—just not the parts I wish were missing. My thoughts are saying: *Did you ask for that? Did you make that happen?* My thoughts are saying: *Why are you such a victim? Why did you let him push you around?* I think of that *hi* and the question mark—how can he be so casual? How can he even dare speak to me? Did I get it wrong? But there is no mistaking this horrible feeling that creeps over me when I let myself think about it. I know that I will never forget this feeling. I *hate* this feeling. I had hopes about falling in love and doing all that stuff and it being amazing and perfect, not being pushed around in a dark alley.

There are only a few more days to make that phone call. Right now all I can think of doing is hiding under my duvet and waiting for this nightmare to be over.

—*Dear oh dear, you look terrible.*
—*Lovely to see you, too, Mr. Cowell.*
—*Was that sarcasm, Katie? My, my, don't get too confident now, the*

audience won't like it.

—I couldn't care less what the audience likes. And it's Kass.

— Fascinating. You're not going to sing for me today, are you?

— Nope.

— Thank heavens. It'll be painful enough to hear you on Saturday.

—It'll be more painful for me than it will be for you.

—I beg to differ.

—So do I.

—I beg to differ more.

—Mr. Cowell, you're really immature for a filthy rich music veteran.

—Don't call me a veteran. Makes me feel old.

—You are old.

— I'm never going to put you through to boot camp if you keep insulting me.

— I don't want to go to boot camp.

— Uh, why are you auditioning, then?

— For my dad.

— Oh, sweet. Sweet, and yet a complete waste of everyone's time. Especially mine.

— Whatever. I've got enough going on without your charming comments getting in my way. I've got to do something for my brother.

— Oh, yes? Hopefully something that doesn't involve singing.

— I've got to save him from a gang of thugs.

— You seem perfect for the job, I must say.

— It's just a phone call. Even a monkey could do it. You could do it.

— I wouldn't be too rude to me, darling; you've been hemorrhaging friends recently without even trying. What's that all about?

– *Only one friend.*

– *You sure about that?*

– *Completely. Umm, I think. I bet you haven't got* any *friends.*

– *If I wanted friends, I'd buy a few.*

– *Where from?*

– *Bloomingdale's. Or perhaps Barneys, if I were in New York.*

– *Good one, Mr. Cowell.*

✳ *Chapter Twenty* ✳

Losing My Friends, My Mind, My Cool . . .
At Least I've Still Got My Hair

It is Friday morning; I am on the bus. Everything that's happened lately seems to have suckered itself onto me like those mollusks that stick to rocks. Limpets, they're called—I only know that because we studied it in Biology on Wednesday. Otherwise I'd have forgotten. It's a shame I can't just forget what I want to forget instead.

Limpets can stay attached even when a massive wave washes over them. And if they leave the rock, they have a way of returning to the exact same spot when they want to. The spot is called a "home scar." So, even if I manage to get rid of some or all of my limpets, will they always come back to haunt me? I ponder this until Izzy sits herself down in front of me as usual.

"You look exhausted," she says, which is ironic because she looks like death warmed over (though still willowy and gorgeous).

"Dad's got me rehearsing around the clock. I think I actually hate my favorite KT Tunstall song," I say.

"Hmm, maybe you should have picked a song you already hate. Like Aversion Therapy."

"Never heard of them."

"It's not a band, Kass. It's a type of therapy. Like, if you hate spiders, they'll put you in a room with a hundred of them, and eventually you end up loving them."

"Where do they get a hundred spiders from? Sounds suspicious to me."

"OK, maybe not a hundred, but a lot. Or maybe it's just one spider, but you have to have it on the tip of your nose for ten hours or something." Izzy makes her fingers wriggle like spider legs and runs them up her face and mimes a scream and we both laugh. I can't remember how we got on to spiders but it feels nice to laugh with her; it feels like it's been a while.

"What's your excuse, then?" I say, mid-giggle.

"For what?"

"For looking like you haven't slept." Her smile drops off. "I meant it nicely," I add. Obviously I should never speak.

"I'm fine. So what are you up to this weekend?" she says. She looks eerily expressionless now.

"Are *you* pissed off with me now? Sorry, Izz. I didn't mean it. You said I looked exhausted so I was just . . . oh, never mind." I realize midsentence that I don't want to get into another argument so I just drop it. "I'm pretty busy this weekend, actually."

"That's nice," she says, with so much sarcasm I almost feel like rekindling the argument. Almost. Instead I just stay quiet and lean my head on the window and stare out of it and drift far,

far away. Izzy turns slightly away from me and looks toward the front of the bus.

"Here comes Char," she says, and I sit bolt upright.

"Did you know she was coming today?"

"Yeah, she told me on the phone last night."

I feel a sudden rush of jealousy when I think about Izzy and Char all cozy on the phone. All week I've been so busy rehearsing with Dad, or plotting this insane chickening-out thing with Raff, that I haven't had a chance for our usual girly chats, or even texts. Not that Char is even speaking to me, but I've still got Izzy, don't I? *Don't I?*

"Why didn't you tell me?" I whisper as the bus doors hiss open.

"Tell you what? You mean you haven't called her all week? But I told you she had tonsillitis, Kass. I can't believe you didn't call her."

"Uh, *hello*? Char isn't speaking to me!" And tonsillitis my ass, I might add. And also, *when* did Izzy stop calling me Furby?

"Well, *I* didn't know," Izzy says. "I knew she was upset . . . you *did* make out with her Dream Boy."

"No I didn't! I . . ." But I sense Char in front of me and I don't have time to set Izzy straight on what happened, or why I haven't been able to speak about it, or what Char is *really* angry with me about.

Suddenly I feel like I've already lost Izzy—as if our amazing friendship has been unraveling itself secretly. I don't know how to wind it back up, so I just sit there watching my two supposed best friends having their normal, uncomplicated friendship, while I feel the pinch of those limpets and try very hard not to cry.

A few stops along, we're all quiet. Izzy looks from me to Char, and back to me.

"Are you two ever going to work this thing out?" she says.

"Izzy!" I say.

"Well, it's gone on long enough. Come on. It's just a boy. You can't let him ruin everything for us."

"It's not *just* a boy," I say, but the look Char gives me stops me from going any further. I don't know what to say anymore, to either of them. I can't win. So much for friends. I've got so much on my plate I can barely see over it: the stupid audition (Izzy knows how ill it makes me feel), Mom cheating on Dad (has Char even stopped to think how this might affect me?), That Night (and Char only seeing what she wanted to see, so she can hate me even more), and the phone call. . . .

Here are my two best friends, scowling at me as if I've just started licking the bus seat. I'd like to shout at them, *It's me, Kass! What's happening to us?* But I don't, because I'm scared of being the only one who cares.

It's nearly the end of one of the worst days of my life, and I can't even hope for a better one tomorrow. Izzy and Char and I have done everything we usually do—we walked to class together, we sat together at lunch, we went to our usual place in the far corner of the tennis courts to read magazines, we ran alongside each other in PE—but it was all painful instead of natural. I can't look at Char without thinking about my mom and her dad, and she sure as hell doesn't want to look at me. It's crazy to think that we both know what's going on but neither of us will say it. I'd never have believed we could be like this, but I don't know how to be any different.

I feel as if we all know that our perfect threesome is finished, but nobody knows how to break away. I bet Izzy and Char are just waiting for me to cut loose and leave them.

We're packing our bags with homework for the weekend. I'm already so behind in my classes, but there isn't enough room in my head to worry about that.

"You both have clarinet lessons?" asks Izzy. It might sound like a fair enough question, except for that Char and I have had clarinet lessons every Friday after school for three years, and we are both currently holding our clarinet cases. This is what it has come to: talking to each other like strangers. Char and I mumble replies and exchange very brief glances.

"OK, well, I'm out of here," says Izzy. "Good luck tomorrow, Kass." (At least she remembered.) "See you later, Char." (What? I didn't know they were doing something tonight. My stomach flips.)

"Yep, meet you outside," says Char.

I can't resist. "What's up? Outside where?" I just hope I sound more natural than I feel.

"Movies. We thought you'd be busy rehearsing," Izzy says.

"Yeah, I am." I grab my bag and clarinet case and start to

walk away. "Bye. Have fun," I say with all the enthusiasm I can muster, and I wave with my back to them as I walk out of the classroom feeling like the odd sock at the bottom of the drawer.

All the way across the soccer field to the building where the music lessons are held, my chest aches the way your finger does if you wind a single strand of hair around and around. There's ten minutes till the start of the lesson so I sit on the ledge of a nearby drain, which is only a few inches tall but somehow feels better than parking myself on the ground. I peer into the drain—*whoa!*—it suddenly gurgles and I scramble to my feet, just as Char comes around the corner.

"Um, what are you doing?" she says.

"The drain made a noise."

"Uh-huh."

There's a tomblike silence as I try not to think of all the jokes we might have made about drain noises back in the good old days before Char hated me for all sorts of reasons that I don't deserve.

"Did you practice?" I say, dipping my toe in the icy water that is my former best friend. Clarinet Practice Enforcement (CPE) is the only thing Char's dad and mine have in common (oh, yuck, until now, of course; thanks, Mom!). The dosage they both prescribe is "half an hour every day, before dinner." The crucial difference is that Char makes the clarinet sound warm and chocolaty, whereas I, even after three long years, make it sound like a camel with bronchitis.

"No," she says. This is a bit like discovering that gravity doesn't exist anymore.

"Oh. How come?"

"I just didn't."

I really want to ask her how she managed to get around her dad for the first time ever in her short but immaculate life, but I don't want to bring him up. Char, however, has other ideas.

"I don't do everything my dad says, unlike some people I know."

"Since when?"

"Since whenever."

"Char, sorry, but you *always* do what your dad says. We even joke about it. You know: the Remote Control?"

"Don't trash-talk my dad."

Hold on! Char's the one who made up that nickname in the first place! I remember because Char isn't usually the nick-naming kind, so it was historic when she did.

"I'm not trashing him, calm down," I say. "It's what *you* always say about him."

"Yeah, well, he's *my* dad. I can say whatever I like. But everyone knows you don't slam other people's parents; you just keep your mouth shut."

"Oh, right, like you did the other night when you bitched about my mom?" Shit, this is getting out of control. Stuff is crawling out from underneath the carpet: Brush it back! Brush it back!

"That's different," she says.

"Like how?"

"I can't talk about this, Kass." She's practically foaming at the mouth, but the other clarinet girls are starting to approach so I subtly *shush* her. I'm sure she doesn't want anyone else to know our business any more than I do.

"Don't *shush* me," she says.

"Calm down, Char, I just don't want people to hear what we're talking about."

"Oh, right, typical, it's all about what *you* want."

"What? This is crazy. I haven't even done anything. And you can't blame me for what . . . someone else is doing."

"Someone else, like your mother? No, but as I said, like mother like daughter—taking what isn't yours and then coming up with a bunch of excuses why it's not your fault." (We now have an audience of eight. I don't know why I don't just leave.)

"Char, stop, please."

"Why should I?"

"Because we're friends."

"Right, like you're Izzy's friend, too?"

"Uh, yes, actually, we've been friends since we were four."

"OK, so what's her big issue right now?"

"What big issue? Izzy always has lots of issues, that's just who she is."

"Her parents are getting back together, Kass. And she doesn't know what to do."

"I knew that!"

"Oh, right, so you've been talking to her about it? Comforting her? Being a friend? Do you have even the vaguest idea of how worried and stressed out she is?"

I put my hand over my mouth, maybe because I don't want to know the answer to the question I'm going to ask and I'm hoping Char won't quite hear me.

"Oh, no. Why didn't she tell me it was so bad?"

"I don't know, Kass. Maybe she thought you were too wrapped up in yourself to listen."

I feel like my insides are seeping out and covering the ground, creeping toward the gurgling drain and eight girls with clarinet cases who suddenly know a lot of my business. I decide to run before any more of me escapes.

"You're all talk, Kass." Char's words feel like knives in my back as I run.

I get my usual bus. When it passes the stop where Char usually gets off, I feel a surge like a chemical reaction in a test tube, and I try to make it pass by racking my brains to think of the substances we used in Chemistry last year. Magnesium something and hydrochloric something else: my anger and guilt making a bitter fizz.

Then the bus goes past Izzy's stop and my legs have life in them, as if they want me to get off here and walk to Izzy's house and beg her to forgive me for not paying attention. But the rest of me is lead-filled and I look straight ahead and then try to make myself believe that it's because of the bus pulling away too quickly that I did not get off and go to face my best friend.

I'm a coward. Everything is my fault. If Dad had paid more attention to Raff and less to me; if I had just made Dad happy years ago instead of resisting him all the time and failing at everything; if I had bothered to notice how left out Raff felt. How could I not notice? And, just the same, how could I not notice that Izzy was burdened with something? How did I miss what Mom was up to? How did I misread Cassian so badly?

I have absolutely no idea who I am anymore. Daughter, sister, friend—I haven't gotten any of them right. The least I can do is make the phone call.

I don't know why standing in the street is the right place to do this, but I can't do it at home and there's nowhere else to go. I'm one block away from our street, sitting on a pebble-dashed wall in front of a house that hasn't been lived in for years, with boarded-up windows and gray mesh bolted down over the front door to keep squatters out.

Dialing the number gives me chest pains. I shudder at the thought of how much I would have liked to call him before; how perfect I thought he was, and how grateful I felt for a single word or a flirty smile.

I'd thought that if I never saw or spoke to him again, I could bury what happened that night. I've blanked out things before.

But it's different now. What does it make me if I never say a word about that night? Or if I let my brother get into trouble because I'm gutless?

"Hello?"

"Is this Cassian?"

"Yep, who's this?"

His voice is cheerful. Somehow it makes me lose my courage.

"It's Kass. Kennedy. I need to talk to you about your brother."

My whole body is throbbing with nerves. He must be able to hear the shakiness in my voice.

"Oh, hey, Kass. Um, how are you?"

"Look, your brother is getting himself messed up with some gang and he's trying to take Raff down with him. I need you to speak to him about it. It's really serious, OK?"

"God, what? Slow down. I don't know what you're talking about, Kass."

"Just listen, then."

I know I sound more confident—bossy, even—but I have to keep taking big gulps between each sentence. I tell him all about the gang and Lucas's threats, and I even find myself confessing about Raff's petty criminal ways and the fact that he's always felt ignored by my dad. Then I stop myself before I go any further.

"So that's it. Just . . . deal with it, OK?"

"Um, yeah, sure. I'm sorry about Lucas. He's not a thug or anything; he's just easily led, and Mom's a bit . . . flaky, let's say, so he's just got me."

The way he talks about his brother makes me feel ashamed; makes me forget myself for a minute.

"Oh, right, yeah, I remember you said about your dad leaving when you were little."

"Yeah, that was just *my* dad, though. Luke's got a different dad. We don't hear from him, either."

I'm softening — this isn't right. I don't want to chitchat about Cassian's family or his problems — that isn't what this phone call is about.

"I just want Raff out of it," I snap.

"OK, OK, sorry. I'll talk to Luke tonight. He's in way over his head and it's probably my fault for spending too much time with the band lately."

Everything he's saying makes me remember why I liked him in the first place. And that makes me angry.

"Great, so we have you to thank for my brother nearly getting his head kicked in."

Silence. Except for my heart thumping. And then: "I'll keep him busy from now on. He can come to our jam sessions; hang out with me more. Don't worry, the gang thing isn't happening. No way."

"Fine. Um, thanks."

And then it's quiet between us again. I think I can hear him smoking. I've picked a leaf off the hedge to my left and started making half-moon incisions all over it with my thumbnail.

"Kass? Are you all right?"

"What do you mean?"

"I just mean . . . the other night."

"What about the other night?"

"You were . . . I went a bit far."

It feels like my throat is closing up. "You were a creep," I say. It comes out like a pathetic croak. I've got to pull myself together.

"I thought you liked me."

I feel sick in the pit of my stomach. I wish I hadn't hesitated that night or worried about what he'd think of me. I wish I'd shoved him hard the second it didn't feel right. I wish I had another chance.

"Kass?"

I take a deep breath.

"I did like you. But you shouldn't have done that. I was saying no and pushing you away."

Silence.

"Admit it, Cassian."

"Kass, I'm sorry."

I wish he wouldn't say my name. I'm losing it here. My cheeks feel like they've been sliced down the middle with hot pins as a few tears fall.

"Kass, I really like you, honest. I screwed up. . . . Shit, I really screwed up, Kass. I feel sick when I think about it."

"*You* feel sick! Ha! Then why did you do it?"

"I'm not excusing it, OK? It's just . . . Look, I want to explain but it's never going to come out right."

"Say it anyway."

"Fine. It was a lot of different things. The girl I was seeing last year dumped me because I was . . ."

"Oh, God, you mean you're a serial creep?"

"No! It was the opposite. She thought I was a bit slow in that department, OK? Shit, I can't believe I'm telling you this . . . it was not exactly a great moment in my life, being told I was behind—not that I'm saying that makes the other night all right. This isn't easy to explain."

"Try."

"OK, and then you said that the guy you were going out with was really immature or something—I know you could have meant anything by that but it stuck in my head, and there was that and the vodka and the whole flirtation thing between us and I just wanted to show you how much I was into you and . . . I'm just sorry, OK? Really."

I don't know if it's OK, so I don't want to say it is. I'm so confused. It's like he's two people in my head—I thought the one I was falling in love with was dead and buried after the other night. This phone call can't go on.

"I don't want to talk anymore. Just fix things with your brother. Bye."

"Kass, wait! Hang on. Did you get the pamphlet?"

"What?"

"The information about what your dad's got."

"That was from you?"

I can't believe it. My head feels so messed up. How can he care so much about his brother, and now about my problems, and still be the pushy creep from the alley?

"Yeah. I printed it off the Internet—seemed kosher, so I asked a girl I kinda know who goes to your school to put it in your locker. It was in an envelope, right? Totally private. I didn't take it to your house in case your dad got mad. I just thought . . . you seemed a bit confused about what to do. Look, his illness is not your fault. It's not your responsibility. I just wanted to help."

This can't be real.

"I don't need your help. *You're* the one who needs help."

I hang up, shove my phone in my coat pocket, wrap my arms around myself, and walk quickly. Everything around me has an unreal quality, like I can't trust the trees not to fall on top of me, or the pavement under my feet not to crack and the ground swallow me up. It was so simple when I could just hate him — not that hating him felt like a picnic in the park, but at least I knew what I thought. Who is this girl he "kinda knows" from my school? What if she peeked in the envelope? Is any of this even over?

Suddenly I stop. It's not over — not even the phone call is over. I forgot to tell Cass that I'd overheard all the stuff about the gang, so that Lucas doesn't think Raff ratted him out. But I can't call him back after the way I hung up on him.

Can I?

"Hello?"

"Um, it's me again."

"Hi. Are you OK?"

"Just stop saying that! Ugh. God, this isn't easy for me, you know. I only called back to say that the reason I know all this stuff about the gang is because I was listening at Raff's door. OK?"

"Really? Why were you doing that?"

"Does it matter?"

"No, just doesn't seem your style."

Is it pathetic that I'm secretly pleased he doesn't think that's my style? Especially since I probably *would* listen at Raff's door? *Now* what do I say?

"Could you just make sure that Lucas thinks I did?"

"Sure."

"Swear?"

"You can trust me, Kass. I'm going to fix all of this. Can I call you about it?"

I literally can't answer that. I just stand with the phone hot against my ear, staring at my shoes, just trying to keep my balance.

"Kass, I'll call you."

I hang up.

"You're late, Kassidy," says Dad. He jumps up from the kitchen table and stands there as if he wants to help me out of my school blazer like some butler. I scowl at him, but his expression remains a glazed but jumpy sort of happy. He's going to use every ounce of self-control tonight in case he unbalances my yin and yang before tomorrow's audition.

"How was clarinet practice?" he says.

"Fine."

"Did she keep you back for some reason, is that why you're late?"

"Um, yeah." Is it still a lie if the other person put the thought into your head, I wonder?

"Oh, yes, what for? Does she want you to play lead in the next concert?"

I can't lie that *well.*

"No, Dad. I suck at clarinet, you know that."

"You suck at it, Kassidy? I was hoping you'd have learned by now that you're supposed to blow!" He arches his back as he laughs, and looks over at Mom and Raff sitting in the kitchen. Mom/Judas smiles and Raff doesn't even look up.

"Anyway, come and eat something, Kassidy. You need a good meal tonight. We got Chinese."

"How come we're having takeout?" I look at Mom, but Dad answers just as she opens her mouth to speak.

"Your Mom had to work late today so she got home too late to cook. Here, egg roll?"

I take the egg roll but I can't quite bring myself to sit down in my usual seat between Mom and Dad.

"Had to work late, huh? What for this time?" My voice is already faltering and I sense Raff looking up from his BlackBerry.

Mom fiddles with the back of her hair and says, "Filing."

"Filing what?" I say.

"Does it matter, Kass?" says Mom.

"Yes, it fucking does."

"KASSIDY!" Dad stands up. "Don't *ever* let me hear you speak like that. Do you hear me?"

For the first time since I found out about Mom, I have the

urge to tell Dad. To hell with the consequences. She's making such a fool of him; the fact that he needs absolutely no help to be a fool doesn't make this any easier. She's supposed to love him, warts and all, like I do—we're supposed to have that one thing in common, and here she is sneaking off every day with the nastiest man she could have chosen. Not a better man at all. And underneath it all there is this nagging guilty feeling because of all the times I've wished for a different dad—not a whole new one, but a seriously revised version. I didn't mean it—I want this dad; this dad who is standing over me waiting for me to promise that I will never speak rudely to my unfaithful mother again.

"I hear you, Dad." I sit down and we eat tepid food with splintery chopsticks while Dad talks us through tomorrow's schedule.

"OK, it's seven ten now, so that gives us twenty minutes to eat and digest our dinner before final rehearsal at seven thirty. Half an hour on song one, half an hour on song two, and then shower, followed by twenty minutes of yoga and then a ten-minute meditation before bed at nine thirty sharp . . ."

It's as if Dad has entered a speed-talking competition. He always talks quickly when he's Up, and even more so when he doesn't really want me to hear what he's saying, in case I disagree—which, of course, I do on every conceivable level, but I haven't got the heart to argue the small points. (As for yoga, he thinks I've been pretzeling myself into the lotus position for a couple of years, but it's always been a way to get excused to go upstairs rather than suffer the horror of family life. It's not every fifteen-year-old who sneaks upstairs {not} to do yoga.)

". . . it's very important that you sleep well tonight, Kassidy, so I've taken your iPod—don't get mad, it's just for tonight—and I've gotten you these." He takes a plastic box from his pocket: bright yellow earplugs.

"You should give those to Simon Cowell, not Kass," says Raff.

"Sshh." Dad dismisses Raff without even looking at him, and for the first time I feel what that must be like for my brother. I take the box.

"Your alarm is set to go off at two thirty A.M., so—"

"What? You've got to be kidding me," I say, and to my right Mom starts giggling. "Um, what's so funny?"

"Nothing. It just it seems amusing that of all the things to get angry about . . . never mind, it doesn't matter." She forces her smile to flatten. Ha-ha. I turn my back on her and give my full attention to Dad.

"OK, as I was saying," he says. "Grace and Raff, I've made a banner, and your job is to stand in line with us, holding it, so that we attract the attention of the cameras."

Mom scrapes her chair back to stand.

"Me? I . . . but I didn't think I'd be coming. I mean, I've made plans. I didn't think . . . you don't usually want us there, Paul." She grabs a dishcloth and wipes her hands, then seems to stumble across the kitchen looking for something else to wipe away. Your tracks, maybe, Mom?

Dad looks like Mom just told him there'd be no Christmas this year.

"But I used the king-size duvet cover to make it," he says.

"That was our only one, Paul." She hangs up the dishcloth and grips the back of her chair. "Not that I mind. It's fine. So, Kass, do you want Raff and me there? I just thought . . ."

"*What* did you think?" I snap.

"I'll be there if you want me," she says. Doubtful.

"No, I don't want you." I focus on chopsticking a cashew nut.

"How about me, Kass?" says Raff. Then he mouths when our parents aren't looking: *Did you call yet?*

I nod, and then say: "You're off the hook."

I get a cheesy thumbs-up. It's bordering on cute, but all I can think about is my mother going on some gross date while I'm propping up Dad's mental health by volunteering to do something that has in the past made me so nervous I've wet myself. This feels like a whole new level of betrayal. She must really hate me.

Right then I know that this can't go on. She can't keep doing this. But telling her I know isn't enough — she'll try to wriggle out of it; she'll say I've imagined the whole thing.

I need to catch her in the act.

Poor Dad's still talking like he's been freebasing caffeine.

"OK, Kassidy, it's just you and me. I don't want to risk taking the car tomorrow. I'll be too nervous to drive and you never know when you're going to blow a tire and there might not be anywhere to park even though there are three thousand parking spaces as I discovered when I did a dry run the other day but who knows how many could turn up so I've booked a cab with a very reputable firm."

"Breathe, Dad," I say.

"OK. I've made sure it's a no-smoking car and the driver has a clean license, and he knows the route to the stadium like the back of his hand." Dad looks at me like a puppy who's just discovered he can chase his own tail for fun. He's even panting slightly.

"Good thinking, Dad." This is all just washing over me now. I'm biding my time until I tell him I can't go in the cab with him. Watching Mom carry on with dinner as if she's in the clear has made up my mind—I'm going to show up at Char's house on Saturday morning. Now I just have to convince Dad to let me meet him at the audition.

He opens one of the kitchen cupboards.

"I've packed this cooler full of snacks and drinks that will keep us going. Carrots, oranges, whole-grain cereal bars— I read somewhere that certain vitamins keep the mucous membranes that line your throat nice and healthy." He rubs his neck as he says this, and I'm bursting to ask him how many carrots he thinks it would take to turn my reedy singing voice into something that human beings would actually want to listen to. "And, of course, we've got plenty of water."

"Of course," I say.

"And salt," he adds. As he's checking and rechecking the contents of the cooler, I get up so that I can put some distance between Mom and me while I put this shaky plan into action. I feel conspicuously unnatural.

"SHIT," I say.

"Kassidy! I hope you're not going to swear in front of the judges tomorrow. It's not attractive," says Dad. He's started to clear away the food even though Mom and Raff look like they're still interested in eating it.

"Dad, oh, damn, I don't believe it. I'm going to have to meet you there tomorrow," I say, doing my best frazzled face. Dad speed-walks toward me.

"What? Why? What for? You can't. No." Great, he's taking it well so far.

"It's this thing for school—some of us have been selected for a science bee and we have to practice tomorrow." My voice is shaking; the countertop digs into my back as Dad has me cornered.

"Science bee? You never mentioned this before," he says.

"Well . . . I only got picked yesterday, and it completely slipped my mind because I've been so focused on the audition. It's really good, Dad, only five students in the whole school were chosen. And it goes toward our final grade."

"A school quiz? It doesn't sound anywhere near as important as the audition, Kassidy." He's right, but I know what makes my dad tick and I'm one step ahead of him.

"Not just *my* school, Dad. This is a *national* thing." I try to ignore Raff's look of mock astonishment over Dad's shoulder.

"But still, Kassidy, a science quiz isn't going to—"

"Dad, it's going to be on *TV.*" His face lights up. Bingo. There's a tiny high-pitched voice in my head telling me that at some point he's going to find out that this is a lie, but I'll just have to smooth that over when it happens. For now, he's happy.

"This is wonderful, Kassidy! I had no idea you were such a talent in this area." He turns to Mom. "I *knew* Mensa didn't have a clue what they were talking about." Then he puts his arm around me and jiggles me toward him vigorously.

"Hang on," he says, holding me suspiciously at arm's length. "Shouldn't they have sent me some kind of form to sign? I know what schools are like these days—you need a permission slip to blow your nose."

I'm so close to pulling this off that I've got pure adrenaline coursing through my veins. I feel like I could run a marathon. Or—let's not be silly here—maybe the hundred-yard dash.

"It's upstairs!" I say.

"Well, go get it, then!" he says, and we are both so wide-eyed—him with excitement, me with slight astonishment that I've nearly gotten away with this—that we must look like a pair of excited tree frogs.

I take the stairs two at a time; I'm almost blind from this rare physical exertion but manage to turn on the computer and sweep all the rubble from my desk to the floor to give me room to think. First, Dad breaks a contract; now I'm faking a school form. So I've inherited his hair, ears, and criminal mind—let's hope that's all. Permission forms—how hard could that be? I type *Permission Form* at the top, put it in bold, and underline it. Yes! It looks authentic!

I'm so deep into my genius scheme that I don't notice the figure at my side until it coughs.

"Wah! Oh, it's you. Go away, Raff, I'm busy."

"I just thought you might need this."

He's holding a stack of paper. And not just any paper. No, it's official St. Agatha letterhead. How in the world did he get his grubby little hands on *that*? I freeze with anticipation. The old Raff would have waved it in front of my face and then set it on fire right before my eyes. But this Raff smiles, slips one sheet into my printer, puts the rest on the desk, and leaves the room without another word.

I take it all back! Cynical no more! I believe in crop circles, alien abductions, poltergeists, the afterlife, and even in mascara that lengthens lashes by up to twenty times with a special conditioning ingredient! I believe in miracles!

Ten minutes and two iffy printouts later I'm heading back downstairs. I pause on the landing to catch my breath and overhear Raff telling Dad that the reason I'm taking so long is that I've had a bad reaction to the cashew nuts and am on the toilet.

I decide not to be annoyed that his cover-up is gross.

"Sorry about that," I say, entering the kitchen rubbing my stomach.

"Kassidy! Are you OK? You look OK!" Dad is frantic.

"I'm fine, Dad."

"No more nuts, you hear me? I didn't realize you were so sensitive."

"Yeah. Me, neither." I glance at Raff and he winks. "Anyway, here it is." I hold the form out a little ways and then put it back by my side.

"Well, I'd better sign off on it, then," says Dad, and I hand it to him upside down, as if stalling for just a few more seconds can help me now.

About a week passes in complete silence. And then:

"Good grief," he tuts. "That science teacher of yours needs to use a dictionary. Look at these spelling errors." I take a look. Whoops. Apparently I'm supposed to show up at the science *departement* tomorrow for *practce* and might be *appeering* on *televison*. "But it does sound like an experience we can't let you miss out on," he says. Sometimes it works in my favor that Dad is blind to my flaws.

Now he slopes over to the sofa and slumps down.

"What are we going to do about *The X Factor*, Kassidy?"

"Hold on a minute," says Mom, still over at the table. All three of us turn sharply: The tone of her voice is different, commanding. It doesn't take a genius to figure out where she's picked *that* up.

"What is it?" says Dad.

"I just think we need to consider what Kass wants, Paul. Is she really going to feel like dashing from a televised science quiz to a televised audition? Let's let *her* make the decisions here." It's like *Invasion of the Body Snatchers*. What's she going to come out with next? *Where ya gonna go? Where ya gonna run? Where ya gonna hide?* It's like having Remote Control Graham actually in the room. I feel oddly powerful knowing that she has no clue what I'm really up to. She's about to seal her own fate.

"Yes, let's let *me* make the decision," I say. I sit next to Dad and put my arm around him. "It's fine, Dad. I can meet you in line." I give Mom a warning glance not to interrupt again. She looks so worried about me. Oh, sure, *now* she's worried. It's Dad she should be worried about. And herself.

"There's a subway to the stadium and you know how long it's going to take to get inside and get a number and everything—it's probably best if I'm not out in the cold air all that time."

"She's right, Dad," says Raff. I could almost get to like him. "Plus, if Kass is concentrating on science all day she won't have time to get nervous about the audition. And you know what happens when she gets nervous. Better bring a mop."

Ah, so he's still Raff underneath this strange new disguise.

"I suppose . . . ," says Dad. "You promise you'll come straight to the stadium afterward? But how will you find me?"

"Easy. Cell phones."

Mom comes over to our cozy gang of three.

"So everyone's happy?" she says.

The feel of her behind me makes my skin crawl. Dad looks at me, all serious, and then his face breaks into a huge smile.

"I'm so proud of you, Kassidy," he says. I hug him quickly before he sees how guilty I look, and how much he breaks my heart.

—*You again. What, couldn't find anyone else to hang out with?*

—*Of course I could. I can't choose my dreams, you know. They just happen. You're the last person I want to spend time with, remember?*

—*Darling, I may be the only person left who's still listening to you.*

—*Umm, no.*

—*I beg to differ. Char obviously can't stand the sight of you. Izzy didn't even tell you she was majorly stressed out over her parents. Raff's only using you. Your mother's too busy being amorous. And your father—well, he's never listened to you.*

—*Guess so.*

—*Oh, no, don't get all glum on me now.*

—*I'll try not to. Mr. Cowell?*

—*Yes, Kass?*

—*I'm scared.*

—*Of me?*

—*No. Funny, you're about the only thing I'm not scared of.*

✳ Chapter Twenty-one ✳

Marriage Counseling for Beginners

I'm on Char's street, shrouded between a parked car and a brambly hedge, and slightly overdressed for spying in my audition outfit: fitted Rolling Stones T-shirt featuring giant red sparkly lips, faux fur black vest, skinny jeans, and ankle boots, with huge hoop earrings that keep getting tangled in my hair, and plenty of face on. I've overdone it with the lip gloss—I feel like I've dipped my mouth in a jar of honey.

While I'm wiping it off with a tissue, I spy Char and Izzy leaving Char's house. They walk arm in arm away from me, one about a foot taller than the other, deep in the excited chatter of pre-shopping-trip girls. That used to be a three-of-us ritual, every Saturday morning.

My phone vibrates in my back pocket. It'll be Dad wanting to give me some last-minute science facts or to tell me again not to swear on TV.

It's not Dad. It's Cassian. I don't know what to do—where's

the PAUSE button? I need time to think about whether to answer.

Too late: It goes to voice mail.

"Hi, Kass, it's just me. I wanted to talk to you about the Lucas thing. Call me. Um, please. OK. Bye."

He sounds kind of nervous on the message, and it reminds me of that time he stumbled on the curb outside my house. It makes me think that I'm always so preoccupied with my own stumbling that I forget that other people might not find life any easier than I do.

I'm calling him.

"Kass?"

"Yep. Hi. I got your message."

"Great. So I spoke to my brother. It got a bit out of hand, but everything's cool now."

"What do you mean, it got out of hand?"

"Um, he punched me." He kind of laughs. "Really hurt, actually, but I think he just needed to do it."

"God. Um, OK, and then what?"

"So then we talked a lot. I won't bore you with the details but I asked him to join the band—kind of an assistant roadie—and he swears he's not getting involved in the gang. I'm gonna keep a closer eye on him. So, are we cool?"

"What do you mean?"

"I dunno. Are you OK about this Raff and Lucas thing?"

"Sure, yes. I'm fine. Thanks for putting a stop to it before it went too far."

And then I cringe at the double meaning of my words. And then it's awkward. He says: "Are you at home?"

"Yep. Are you?"

"Yep, just leaving—for the audition. You?"

"Yep, just leaving." I am a professional liar.

I peer around the parked car and imagine him in his house, maybe in his room, maybe at his drum kit, speaking to me.

"Kass? Is there any chance we could . . . ?"

"I don't think so."

That's hard to say when I still have feelings for him, but I know it's right. I can't go back. He's not the Bad Guy I thought he was, but I can't just forget it.

"But, Cass? Thanks for the pamphlet and everything. I think you're a . . . nice guy."

"I'm really glad you think so. But, really really never? For us, I mean?"

"How about friends?"

I wait about a week for him to answer.

"Friends is good. OK, gotta go. I guess I might see you in line, right?"

I laugh. "That seems likely with about a million people there."

He laughs. Maybe we really will be friends. I could use some, that's for sure.

"See ya, Kass."

"See ya, Cass."

We both laugh as we hang up.

About a minute later it's back to reality as I hear the *clip-clip-scrape-clip* of high heels, and I know without looking that it's my mother. I peer around. She opens the gate and walks up the path to Char's house as if she owns the place. He must have been waiting for her by the door because she walks right in. I feel like my insides are on fire. What am I doing here? I am so riddled with nerves and bursting with purpose: This could go either way—*I* could go either way. Run away, or deal with it.

I'm at the front door, breathing in through my nose and out through my mouth—finally Dad's breathing exercises are coming in handy. The doorbell chimes in that familiar way and I have to steady myself by holding on to the porch.

I know Graham will answer. I bet he'll pretend he doesn't know who I am. As I wait I mutter an imaginary conversation to calm my nerves:

— *You're one of Charlotte's friends?*
— *Well, I'm not the mailman, Mr. Roebuck.*
— *I'm sorry, but are you sure we've met?*
— *Tell you what, add twenty years and imagine me in something beige from Talbots. That might ring a bell.*

But that's where the script ends; everything else I say will have to be improvised. I only know that I cannot, I must not, cry or come across like a baby, or have him pity me—I've got to stay in control and state my points.

This is taking forever; I dread to think why. As I crouch down and look through the mail slot, I get an eyeful of navy blue trousers and spring upright as the door opens.

"Oh. Kass." He doesn't sound cold and hard like normal; there is warmth in that just-seen-a-ghost expression. It makes me feel sick.

"Can I come in?" I say. I'm pretty surprised by how forceful I sound.

"Charlotte isn't here."

"I know. I've come to see you." I try to look over his shoulder when I hear the sound of the toilet flushing, and he moves to block me.

"Kass, I think you should go," he says, putting a hand up like a power-crazy traffic cop.

"Is that my mom?" I try to step forward, but he puts his arm on the door frame, so I hang on to it and try to budge him. "Mom!"

She comes out of the downstairs bathroom where I drank the vodka and ate the Christmas fruitcake. She clutches her chest when she sees me and stumbles back against the wall, letting out a kind of tragic moan. Then, as if she's been reprogrammed by the Robot Master, she straightens up and smoothes her hair and comes toward the door.

"Kass, hi, what a surprise. I came to pick you up but you weren't here!"

Is she kidding? She must think I was born yesterday.

"I never said I was going to be here."

Remote Control's arm is still blocking me, until Mom comes right to the door. The sight of them together makes my knees buckle.

"Oh, didn't you? I could have sworn you said you were heading to Char's right before the science quiz. And here you are. So, shall we go?"

She's unbelievable; except she's not, she's good, she's really good — if I didn't already know for sure what a two-faced liar she was, she'd have convinced me.

"I never said I was heading to Char's." I can't quite bear to blurt out that I know everything; slow and painful seems preferable somehow. "I'm supposed to be meeting Dad for the audition, remember?"

"Of course you are! Well, come on, we'd better get going. I've got the car, so I'll race you over there. Thanks, Graham, we'd better be off."

He looks bewildered. She grabs her coat and bag and comes toward me, but this time *I* block the way with my arm on the door frame.

"That was pathetic," I say, almost at a whisper.

"Come on, Kass," she says, pretending she didn't hear me, "let's get going."

"No," I say, and her chin trembles and she puts her hand over her mouth and runs back into the house, crying.

We're at the kitchen table, the three of us. I feel like Mom and Char's dad are a unit, and I'm the outsider; maybe because they're sitting in identical positions with their hands clasped together, placed on their lips, and their elbows on the table, and both staring at me. I almost wish Char was here. Or rather, I wish Char was here and that she didn't hate me.

"Well, is one of you going to speak?" I say. I can't believe how angry I feel; I'm not even close to crying.

"Kass . . . ," begins Char's dad, lowering his clasped hands.

"Not you!" I snap, and then I look at Mom. Her whole face starts twitching and she bursts into tears again.

"Oh, darling, I'm so sorry. I never wanted this."

"What? To get caught? Well, you did a pretty shitty job, then, because *I* know, *Raff* knows—"

"Raff? Oh, God, please no." Mom turns briefly to Char's dad, and for a second I get distracted by the jealous thought that now she's more concerned about Raff's feelings than mine. But then I feel protective of him again, and the jealousy gets shunted back where it belongs.

"And Char knows," I say to her dad. He closes his eyes and lowers his head and I notice for the first time that he has a bald spot. My dad doesn't have a bald spot. He doesn't wear polyester navy blue pants and nasty gray shoes, either. *And* he doesn't have hairy knuckles. If it's possible, I have even less respect for my mother now.

I'm starting to get annoyed by how quiet they're being. I don't know what I expected (that's what happens when your natural tendency is to do things without thinking them through, I suppose), but the rage bubbling inside me doesn't seem compatible with how calm they seem, despite my mother's quivering chin and tendency to let out little bursts of gentle crying.

"So, what is this . . . *this*?" I say, wagging my finger back and forth between them. I know how bold I must sound, though inside I'm still wondering when I'm going to get yelled at for being so disrespectful. But they're both so meek, so guilty, it's like I have no choice.

They shrug awkwardly as if they have itching powder in their matching beige sweaters. Then Mom straightens up and sniffs as if she's done with crying and has pulled herself together. At last it seems like I might get some answers.

"To be honest, Kass, I don't know."

Char's dad looks at her as if this is news to him. Mom won't meet his gaze.

"I wasn't really thinking about what it was . . . is . . . was, whatever, sorry. Sorry, Graham."

"Don't apologize to him! Why would you apologize to him? I can't believe this. What's the matter with you?"

"Don't speak to me like that, Kassidy." She smacks the table and stands.

"It's Kass."

"It's KASSIDY, actually. I'm your mother and that's the name I gave you."

Graham gets up and, with all ten fingertips placed lightly on the table as if he's afraid it might levitate, he speaks very calmly. "I'm going to leave you two for a minute. I'll be in the living room."

Mom doesn't bat an eyelid; she's still fuming over what I said. Unbelievable! She has the nerve to get angry at me. I didn't even know she had . . . *nerve*. Well, guess what? Me, too.

"Don't shout at me." I stand so we're eye to eye. "*You're* the one who's betrayed everyone. *You're* the one who's ruined my friendships and let your children down and cheated on Dad. How could you do that to him? He loves you."

"No, he doesn't! He doesn't even know I'm there. I'm invisible; I'm nothing. You don't know what you're saying. You don't know anything about this. What do *you* know about marriage?"

"Uh, I know you're supposed to be *faithful*. I know you're not supposed to *screw* your daughter's best friend's dad."

The slap across my face and the look of rage on Mom's face stops me dead.

"Oh, God, I'm sorry, Kass," she says. "I'm so sorry, but you're not being fair—I know how awful this must seem, but you don't understand. You *couldn't* understand what it's like to be me."

I just hold my cheek as my eyes fill with tears while she keeps on talking: "I go to work every day and I'm the drudge, the one who does what nobody else thinks themselves low enough to do, and I don't get thanked for it. Then I come home and I tread on eggshells in front of your father in case he . . . flips out. And meanwhile I'm getting it in the neck from you and your brother for not buying the right potato chips or cooking the right dinner or ironing the right shirt, or for nagging, or for just being a bad mom. And you know what, Kass? Just for a change I wanted to spend some time with a grown-up who doesn't really *need* me but really *wants* me. And who thinks I'm OK. I'm not so bad."

She slumps back into the chair and resumes her position of elbows on table, clasped hands in front of mouth. She's shaking.

"Please, Kass, sit down."

But what could I possibly say? And how much more can I bear to listen to? I can't fix this. I don't know why I thought I could.

Without another word I walk out of the kitchen and down the hall, catching a glimpse of Graham standing pensively by the mantelpiece and a photograph of Char. I walk out, leaving the door wide open.

Somewhere in the city, in a long, long line, Dad is waiting.

✳ *Chapter Twenty-two* ✳

This Train Terminates at . . .

It may be because I've used up my entire sense of purpose that it takes me two hours to reach the subway station — a fifteen-minute walk, usually. It's as if there's an invisible force field around it, repelling me. I've been into three clothing boutiques and two bookshops. I've cried in the bathroom at Starbucks and fixed my makeup in the mirrors of Sephora.

Now I'm down here in the station. What a milestone. I've been standing in front of the subway map long enough to memorize the whole thing; I can't walk away until I'm absolutely sure which route to take. This way takes ten stops with two transfers; that way takes nine stops with three transfers. Just when I think I've decided and let my eyes drift up the track, self-doubt creeps back in and I'm looking at the map again. How many stops was it this way? Did I count right? I do this until it gives me a headache, and then I give up and decide to sit on a bench and imagine the conversation I'll have to have with Dad when I finally find him in line.

I take out my cell for the first time since I talked to Cass and check the clock; I have a few hours before the auditions close. I can't even bear to think what state Dad must be in—him and that king-size duvet with KASSIDY KENNEDY HAS THE X FACTOR painted on it—but the one, two, three, four phone beeps announcing new messages is just a small clue. Five. Six, seven. Eight? Oh, no.

There are eight new voice mail messages, from twenty-five calls. There are six texts that I allow my eyes to graze over but don't quite take in. I could have written them myself, after all:

You promised me.

I trusted you.

You are letting me down.

I am hurt.

I am worried.

WHERE ARE YOU?

233

He's going to be even more furious when he sees what I'm wearing, unless the judges are looking for a singer who can't sing *but* still has the balls to wear a T-shirt that evokes possibly the greatest band of all time. My only consolation is that I'm not even a tiny bit scared of meeting Simon Cowell, if I even get that far, which, knowing my dad, I will (he'll use one of his many resources: puppy-dog eyes, guilt trip, lame joke collection, wallet).

After a while I realize that I am tugging clumps of hair from the nape of my neck. And that this is something I've been doing a lot lately. I freeze, completely freaked out, because I know it's something I do every time I'm stressed, but it's knocking on the door of Casa Kass, wanting to be let in, wanting to make itself at home in my head and become a normal part of my life.

I think back to the pamphlet:

Self-harm may become a factor. This can include cutting, burning, hair-pulling, and eating disorders.

Is that what's happening here? Could this be the start of becoming the one in ten?

Suddenly this whole thing once again seems like the wrong thing to do. But am I just scared of the audition or of my dad or of something even scarier—of my own mind? Of the nameless chemicals that act without known cause and have no cure? I pull my sleeve over my hand, bunch it into my fist, and exhale into it.

The stress moves to my left leg, which becomes possessed by a frantic jiggle. At the sound of a familiar voice I turn to the stairs leading up from the platform. The jiggling stops. I could pick those long legs out of a lineup; they are Izzy's, and she's shouting good-bye to Char.

"Take care, babe!" she calls.

I panic and get up from the bench and face the map again. What am I doing? We've been best friends since we were four. She's so familiar to me I sometimes even forget her name. Does that make sense? Oh, God, do I ever make sense? I need Izzy. And here I am contemplating avoiding her on a subway platform. I sense her pass.

"Izz."

"Kass! You scared me. What are you doing here? Shouldn't you . . . ?"

"Yep, I should. I'm late. Just on my way now."

"Oh. Well, good luck, babe. I'm off to the other platform. Probably see you . . . Monday, I guess?"

This is awful. It's as if we're reading from the wrong script and stumbling over the words because they don't feel true to us. I could walk away now and I wouldn't have to face the resentment I feel because she's just spent the morning with someone who hates me, or the guilt I feel because I know I've been a bad friend to her.

"Wait," I say, grabbing her arm and then feeling like I've invaded her space and letting go. "Wait. How's everything?

How's stuff with your parents?" The roar of the subway wipes out the last half of my sentence.

"Better get your train, Kass."

"Doesn't matter, I'll get the next one. Let's sit here for a minute."

"But what about your dad, and the audition?"

"It's OK. Just sit." I go to the bench and pat a space next to me. She sits a little farther away than where I patted. "So, your parents?"

She breathes out heavily and her wiry frame seems to collapse a bit.

"It's . . . weird," she says. "You think you know how things are, and then it all gets turned upside down."

"I know what you mean," I say. She smiles politely, but this is not the time to make her see that I really do. "What does your therapist say?"

"She says I have to let my parents make their own mistakes."

I chew on that, willing my mind to focus on Izzy's problem instead of relating it to my own. I manage a feeble, "Ironic." And a shrug.

The subway roar doesn't have anything to wipe out this time, but we look at each other and I wrinkle my nose and shake my head. When the train stops and the doors open I say, "I'll get the next one."

"OK, if you're sure," she says.

"Absolutely."

The train pulls away, and I swallow a lump made entirely of guilt at the thought of my dad still standing in line.

"Why didn't you tell me how much this was upsetting you?" I say. "Char mentioned it."

"I was going to tell you. I tried to, but other things kept getting in the way and you've just seemed a bit . . . somewhere-else-ish."

"I know, I'm sorry. So, will you tell me now?" I give her this look that for an instant sends a chill down my spine—and then I realize that it is the look Dad gives me when he wants forgiveness.

"They've been really open about how they feel," she says. "They want it to be a new start for all of us, but they're being *really* considerate of *my* feelings. . . ."

"That's good, isn't it?"

"It's nauseating, Kass. They're saying they won't get back together if it's going to mess me up."

For a moment I can't understand why she doesn't just tell them not to and be done with this stress, but then it clicks.

"Oh. So basically it's *all* up to you."

"Yep. I've been given the opportunity to either totally upset their new true love plans, which involve Mom singing sappy songs again and not wanting to stab every man she meets, and Dad losing Miss Carphone Warehouse and trading in the Porsche and picking flowers for my mom in the park, OR totally ruin *my* life by watching them realize it was all a huge mistake because they're still the same two people who can't live together for more than ten minutes without starting World War Three and then tearing each other apart for the second time and playing tug-of-war with me." Finally she breathes.

"Wow," I say, oh-so-helpfully. "What is wrong with our parents?"

"Yours are OK, aren't they?"

"Not really. No. Not at all."

"I didn't know."

"Neither did I, until recently. Anyway, what do you think you'll do?"

"I don't know. I mean, shouldn't I want my parents to be happy, and together? What's wrong with me?"

"Oh, Izz, there is *nothing* wrong with you. You're amazing." I shift along the bench and put my arms around her. "I'm so sorry for being a crap friend, Izzy. I'll make it up to you."

"It's OK, Kass." She laughs, and it's warm and easy. We come apart, but we're sitting close now. "I know you can get a bit distant when your dad's making you jump through hoops."

"It's not that, though. Can we go back to your place and I'll tell you about it?"

"'Course we can. I'd love that. But what about the audition?"

I think about the pamphlet again: *The child is not to blame for the parent's disorder. It is the adults who must be the "helpers." Not the kids.*

"Come on." I pull her up and she towers over me, my willowy, beautiful best friend. "Oh, and Izz, when did you decide to stop calling me Furby?"

"Never. Come on, lil' Furby, *wee-tee-kah-wah-tee.*"

"I can't believe you remember Furbish!" I pretend-punch her and we giggle like the children we were when that joke was born.

I don't know if I'm being brave or a coward, but I do know that linking arms with my best friend and going to the other platform feels like the right thing to do.

Chapter Twenty-three

The Blame Factor

It's dark and I'm soaked with the kind of rain that doesn't feel like it's falling but dancing in midair, tickling the skin on my face and drenching me in secret.

I've taken the shortcut, but there's just an empty space where the Stamping Man usually is. I wonder where he goes when he's not here. Who looks after him?

At Izzy's place, hours earlier, I sent a text message to Dad to say that I wasn't coming to the audition and that I'd explain everything when I saw him back home. Then at Izzy's I talked and talked, and Izzy talked and talked, and by the end of it we were both sure we'd worked everything out about our parents, like taking a bowl of spaghetti, untangling it, and lining up the stretched-out strands. But now that I'm going back to face them, it's just spaghetti again.

It's eleven o'clock when I walk up the front path, an hour after my usual curfew, but I figure that since I'm already up to my eyes in trouble, I might as well go completely under. All the way home I tried to put what I've done into words:

I didn't show up at an audition that I never wanted to go to in the first place.

It doesn't sound so bad, put like that, and it's gotten me all the way to my front door. But the second I walk in the weight of it weaves its way into my lungs, and my heart sinks when I see Dad at the kitchen table. His head is bowed, and he doesn't flinch even when I shut the front door and let my keys clatter on the hall table.

He's wearing a suit. I focus on that in the silence — I didn't see him leave this morning and for all I know he'd been sleeping in those awful ironed jeans that have become his uniform for the last few weeks. The suit somehow makes me all the more sorry to have hurt him. He tried *so hard*, again, and I didn't try at all.

"Hi," I say. He remains slumped but moves a little to show that he's heard me. Completely refusing to notice that he has his hideous white running shoes on with the suit, I go to the tea-kettle and start to make him a small cup of consolation — with milk and two heaping teaspoons of sugar. There are Kit Kat bars in the cupboard but that feels too obvious, as if I really thought that he'd be OK if I "gave him a break." (What, rather than a breakdown?) I hear him light up a cigarette and notice that there's a saucer in front of him overflowing with butts. He only ever smokes inside when he's . . .

"Where's Mom?" I say, a tiny bit louder than the gurgle of the kettle.

"On her way back from Maria's." He repeats Mom's lie flatly, down into his chest, as if hypnotized by the purple swirls on his tie. "One of their girl nights. Raff's staying at a friend's house."

"Who? Lucas?"

"Possibly."

So that's that, then—Raff and Lucas are friends again. I helped do that. Even the Cass thing doesn't feel so bad anymore. In theory, my shoulders should feel 50 percent less weighed down, because two out of my four problems are no more. I don't. I'm so weighed down I'm sensing the beginnings of a hump.

I know this version of Dad so well. He is catatonic with disappointment. Over me. He is on his way to Planet Down.

I set the mugs of tea on two of the red vinyl apples and sit next to him.

"Have you eaten?" I say. He briefly glances at the cooler and nods. I continue. "It was cold today. Did you have a coat on?" He shakes his head. "You should have taken one." I don't know why I'm saying what I'm saying, so I shut myself up by drinking too hot tea in tiny slurps that seem deafening in this heavy atmosphere.

Suddenly he scrapes the chair back, chucks his pack of cigarettes on the table, and starts to leave.

"I'm going to bed," he says.

"Dad, wait. Don't leave it like this."

"Like what, Kassidy?"

"Just sit down, please."

"I'm tired. I have nothing to say to you right now." He stares at me with bloodshot eyes. "Good night."

I'm lying here, awake, and I don't know how long I've been staring at my lamp, or when I switched it on, or if I've been to sleep at all. Through the skylight I see it's light outside.

I drag myself up, feeling desperately heavy. Everything is hard work: pulling my sweatshirt off the chair and over my head (the chair falls over), putting on my slipper socks (I fall over), pulling a face wipe out of the pack to get rid of yesterday's makeup (a whole clump of them come out). Then I stand on my side of the door, wondering what to expect when I go downstairs.

Before I leave I take the pamphlet out of the book and lay it on my desk. Faceup. There it is: what we're dealing with in this house. We can't hide it, or hide from it, anymore. In my sweatshirt pocket I have Izzy's mom's business card.

Dr. Barbara Franklin, PhD, LCSW
Family Therapist

By the bottom of the little flight of stairs that leads to my bedroom I can hear television noise, and I lose my nerve as I picture Dad in his gray tracksuit, flicking channels, smoking, drinking tea. He'll be Somewhere Else, and heading Who Knows Where. Part of me wants to go back upstairs and crawl under the duvet. But the part of me that wins, by a hair, is the part that wants to avoid there being two of us in this household who turn to mush when the going gets tough.

I look for Dad in the armchair but he isn't there. Mom's on the sofa. She looks completely exhausted. I shudder to think why, only she doesn't look happy.

"Where's Dad?"

"Oh, morning, Kass, I didn't see you there."

"Uh-huh. Where's Dad?"

"He ran out for some milk."

"Really? He went out?" I rush to the front door. "Shouldn't someone go with him? What if he has one of those manic attacks? How could you let him go out by himself?" I start to pull off the slipper socks and hunt around for suitable shoes, sobbing and utterly frustrated by how tired I feel and how alone I am in this. *Where are my shoes?*"

"Kass! Calm down, honey! He's OK." She comes toward me and I plunge my feet into the only shoes I can see, which happen to be Dad's ridiculously white sneakers.

"How can he be OK?" I push her back from me. "Don't come near me, I don't want you near me." Oh, God, but I do, I want someone to hold me and let me cry. I want my old, reliable mom.

"Kass, please listen. Your dad is fine. He was upset about the audition but I think he's coming to terms with it, and with how you feel."

I stop crying and wipe my face with my sleeve.

"Really? How?"

"I don't know, Kass. We can't predict these things. All I can say is that it's not your fault when Dad gets low—and if I've allowed you to believe otherwise then I'm truly, truly sorry."

I just sniff, and still can't quite bear to look her in the eye. I step out of the shoes.

"Um. OK."

"If it helps, he's not wearing the gray tracksuit today." I can tell by her voice that she's smiling. If she thinks she's getting a smile out of me, she can think again. "Come and sit down. Please, Kass. I know I've let you down. I need to talk to you about what to do next."

I shuffle toward the armchair, my nose and eyes throbbing from the crying, and feel like I'm about to hear the reading of someone's will: *To my daughter, Kassidy, I bequeath a life of twisted lies and cover-ups while I sashay off to do despicable things with her best friend's creepy dad.*

"Your dad and I have been talking since last night. I haven't told him yet about Graham but I'm going to."

"You're *what*? You can't tell him *that*! That'll kill him! Worse, it'll make him go completely nuts. You just can't do it. You can't! Look, I've got Dr. Franklin's card—I was going to give it to Dad. She can get him an appointment with someone. But you can't tell him what you've done—he'll crack and then I'll never convince him to try to get some help. Haven't you done enough?"

"Kass, calm down."

"And *stop* telling me to calm down!"

"Well, I've got to! I'm your mother!" She stands over me; she's finally lost her cool, like she did in Char's kitchen. "Look, I know I've done this all wrong—I'm not perfect. And I know on the face of it I look like a pretty shitty mother and an appalling wife, but I'm trying here, Kass, I am trying to fix things, and I need one thing from you."

Strangely, I feel calmer. It's a weird kind of "someone is shouting at me and I needed it" calmer. Except that I'm dreading what it is she needs from me.

"Kass, I need you to go to Raff, explain what's happening here today with me talking to your dad about Graham, and how this family goes forward, especially about Dad's health. I need you to spend the day with him—I'll give you money to see a movie, eat, do whatever. You're in charge. I need you to look after each other while I deal with Dad, and then I need you to come home. Can you do that?"

I nod.

"Um, are you leaving us?" I sniff.

"Oh, no, Kass, no. Darling, I'd never leave you."

"Are you leaving Dad?"

"No. I'm going to try to work things out. I mean really try. Is that OK?"

"OK."

She wants to hug me, I can tell, but I'm not ready, so I edge my way out of the armchair and go up to my room to get ready. I have no idea how Mom thinks that Dad will ever get over this, or that they'll ever be normal again, but somehow this feels better than I thought it would; it feels like the right thing is happening. And I have instructions. Easy ones.

When I come back down, Dad still isn't there.

"A pint of milk, you said."

"You know what he's like. He's called me to say he decided to drive to the supermarket and do a whole load of food shopping. Your dad doesn't do things by halves." The way she says that makes it sound as if she still loves him. But then, how could she? And how could they have done it to me and Char? I feel myself harden again.

"When will I get to explain to him about yesterday?"

"Later. It'll be OK. He understands." She's firm, she's kind. I could almost like this New Mom. I just wish I didn't still hate her.

On my way out she asks for the business card.

I don't go to Lucas's house to pick up Raff; the phone calls with Cass were stressful enough without actually running into him. I text Raff and we meet outside the shopping center. He comes toward me, smiling.

"Everything OK with you and Luke?" I say.

"Yeah. Thanks, sis. Luke's brother even said I could be a roadie. We had a wicked night listening to the band."

"Oh, right, so how did they do at the audition?" I sound nonchalant when I say this. Maybe if I sound nonchalant I will start to feel nonchalant. About a decade of hard-core practice should do it.

"Totally slammed. They got through to Cowell and he called them average and a bit greasy."

"Ouch. Harsh." This feels weird, kind of like Simon Cowell has inadvertently defended my honor. "So, you're a roadie. And do roadies live on their BlackBerries and commit credit card fraud?"

"Ha. Maybe I'll break the mold. Anyway, what are we doing here?"

"We need to talk."

"Uh-oh. Is it about Mom and Dad?"

"They don't call you a pint-size Evil Genius for nothing. Come on, I'll buy you a coffee."

"I don't drink coffee."

"Soda, then."

"Nope."

"Chicken soup."

"Hilarious."

"OK, how about a hazelnut hot chocolate with whipped cream and marshmallows and a double chocolate muffin to go with it?"

"Now you're talking."

So my brother and I go to get high on sugar and talk about our messed-up family. Except, before long, Raff seems to lose interest in brooding about what might happen, and instead he starts talking about the past. Fun stuff we've all done together—vacations and random Saturdays—when Dad hasn't been at either end of the pendulum. Things I'd forgotten. In fact, when he starts it's as if he's talking about a completely different family. He even makes it sound as if he and I get along. I sound pretty good in his stories. Most of them, anyway. We're getting along better than we have in years when a text comes.

"It's from Mom." My finger hovers over the button.

"Well, read it!"

"I'm scared to."

"Kass, it'll be fine. Look, they're the adults, we're just the kids—it's not our job to fix everything or blame ourselves for everything. We've got enough going on, right? Just in normal life?"

"Who made you so Oprah all of a sudden?" I say to my Rat-faced Mutant Little Brother, who, I now realize, I wouldn't be without for anything in the world. He looks pretty happy.

The text says:

Coast clear. We've talked. Dad has gone to a friend's
but he's OK. Don't worry. Come home.

All the way home I do the opposite of what Mom said: I worry. I worry about Dad's state of mind, and about which friend's he's gone to—I can't think of any good friends that Dad would turn to over something like this. He's always said he didn't need friends; he had Mom.

Raff automatically takes the shortcut and I'm too caught up in my thoughts to say otherwise, though when we pass the Stamping Man my worry just about quadruples. Is *he* someone's dad? How did he start out? Healthy and happy, or was he always like that, always afflicted by the nameless chemicals that attack at random and for which there is no cure? And is my dad standing in the street somewhere, alone and going mad?

Mom opens the door when we're halfway up the path and Raff runs into her arms. I manage a smile, but once she's promised me another hundred times that Dad's really OK—it turns out he's with Tony Ferrari, of all people—I just want to be alone.

—I'm waiting.

—For what, Mr. Cowell?

—An apology, that's what. I thought we had a date yesterday.

—Yeah, sorry about that, I had a better offer.

— Charming.

— Oh, come on, you only wanted me to come so you could show off a few of those prepackaged barbed comments. I can hear them now: "Utterly, utterly average," "You've got the personality of a candle," "If you're a singer, I'm Tweety Pie."

—You know, I like you less and less.

—I'm not so bad. And I am sorry I couldn't make it to see you. There's just a lot going on now, and chasing someone else's dream isn't at the top of the list.

—*Very profound. But point taken. I suppose you have had a lot on your plate. You did the right thing.*

—*Wow, you almost sound nice.*

—*I am nice!*

—*Yeah, you're OK, Mr. Cowell.*

—*You're OK, too, Kass Kennedy.*

✳ *Chapter Twenty-four* ✳

Let's Face the Music, and Duck

Four days later, I catch two buses to Tony Ferrari's house. On the first bus I cast my mind back a few weeks and wonder what I'd have thought if someone had told me I'd be on my way to visit my dad—who'd left home because my mom had confessed to an affair with my best friend's father—at the home of a Simon Cowell impersonator.

On the second bus I rehearse over and over what I'll say to Dad about leaving him stranded at the *X Factor* auditions. I can't really think about what to say about everything else until we've gotten past that.

Tony Ferrari lives in a new housing development that looks like Legoland, without the cool little people with yellow heads. All the window frames and front doors are bright blue, and each house has two pointy dark green plants on either side of the path. There's nothing to tell them apart, but I spot Tony's house from a mile away because the license plate on his car says SIMON 2.

My dad opens the door. He is unshaven and has dark circles under his eyes, but he smiles and we hug on the doorstep for ages.

"Come in," he says. "Tony's gone out to give us some space."

We step over several pizza boxes to reach the kitchen, which is supremely bare except for brown rings of coffee on nearly every surface and about fifteen unwashed mugs in the sink. Dad suddenly turns around and says, "I should have made lunch. Do you want lunch? I can call for a pizza." He picks up the phone and starts to dial.

"No, Dad!" I take the phone from him. "I don't want to eat. I came to talk."

"Right."

"Let's sit down," I say.

He actually does. I don't want to get giddy with power, but I think this is the first time he's done something I've asked.

He combs his hands through his (seriously unwashed) hair, and then he starts to look twitchy, like something's brewing, working its way out of him, about to explode, and then he gets up again and smacks his hand on the table.

"*Why* didn't you come? *Why?*"

I'm scared, and try not to look at the bead of spit in the corner of his mouth.

"Dad, please."

"Please *what*? I waited and waited for you." He is bright red and standing over me. "I looked like an idiot. How could you do that to me?" All I can see are his bloodshot eyes.

"Just listen to me for once!" I face him head-on, but my voice is shaking.

"No, you listen to me, Kassidy. I was there for hours in that line. I never thought you'd let me down like that — *ever.*" He starts to pace around, miming with his hands as if he's clutching each word, flinging it down, reaching for another, swiping it out of his way. "I got to the front, *finally*, and do you know what I said to them? *Nothing.* I waited in that line in silence most of the night and all day, in *silence*, and when I made it to the desk I said *nothing*. I just turned around and walked back out." He looks at me, getting out of breath, and starts to light a cigarette but can't quite coordinate himself, so he throws the pack across the room. "Do you have any idea how that felt? A thirty-nine-year-old man struck dumb. I was humiliated! I felt like . . . *nothing.*"

I don't know why I thought I could do this. I'm already crying. I don't say a word, just stand and face him. What he's saying doesn't even sound like a huge deal — he was in a line, so what? He got to the end and said nothing, so what? But there is so much more to this. Mom said he was dealing with it and with everything else, but she must have gotten it wrong. I'm scared.

But then he slumps in his chair like a puppet whose strings have been cut. When he speaks again his voice is completely different, low and calm, as if he's playing multiple characters in a play.

"There were thousands there," he says. "People with tents; whole families; such a collection of people I've never seen before.

It wasn't like the other auditions we've been to. People dressed up in silly costumes, people practicing their songs in the open air, talking to one another, waving to the cameras. They were all buzzing. And the more I saw how much they all wanted it, the more I realized how little you do." He sounds so bitter as he looks up at me. "That's true, isn't it?"

Even the gods of sarcasm would frown on me for taking this opportunity, so I simply say, "Yes, it's true."

He looks away again, but this time his shoulders shudder and he cries. It's just for a second, but it's awful.

"I sat on the cooler and waited for you, shifting along as the line moved. I must have overheard a hundred conversations between parents and their teenagers. *Do you think I'll get to sing in front of the real judges, Dad? Will you come in with me, Dad? Can we go through the songs one more time, Dad? Oh, Dad, I'm so nervous!*" He's doing impressions of these kids, in that animated way of his, and I have to bite the inside of my mouth—I feel sick and hysterical at once.

"At first I thought, *That'll be me and Kassidy soon, when she gets here.* But then I heard *your* voice in my head: *I don't want to go, Dad. Leave me alone, Dad. I'm only doing this one last time so you'll stop making me, Dad.* That's what you say, isn't it?"

"Dad, you know it is. I've always said it."

"Yes, yes, I know."

I'm about to speak but I realize that for all his ranting a minute ago he's actually worked it out for himself.

He looks at me again, and this time I know he's not playing

any new character; he's not Dad the Game Show Host, or Dad the Disappointed Parent, or Dad the Charming, Too Cute Child, or even Moody Dad from Planet Down. He's my real dad, the one I knew was buried underneath all that—the dad I put up with all the other dads for.

"You don't want to be a star, do you?"

I shake my head, and allow just a tiny smile.

"You just want to make up your own mind."

I think it's a rhetorical question.

"You want your old dad to butt out."

"Maybe just a bit," I say.

He empties his lungs purposefully. Then he rests one arm on the table, the rest of his body slack, his head too heavy for his neck.

"I was doing it for me," he says, his voice a quiet scraping sound. "When I was ten, my father . . ." His face crumples so that I know what the next word is. But he uncrumples himself and tries again. "My father died, Kass." He clears his throat and shifts away as if he knew I was going to reach for him. Tears are streaming down his face, but he's completely still; he just lets them fall. "He was . . . a very brave man. Firefighter." He laughs a hollow laugh. "Classic hero, right?"

I don't think he wants me to say anything. I am so afraid of what he's about to tell me. I feel like it shouldn't just be me here.

"I never measured up. Of course I didn't! Look at me." He shifts his legs and then his arms, as if he's showing me how defective he is. "My mother took it very badly; it was like she couldn't wait to join him, and the only thing keeping her here was me. She resented me for that, I think." He stops. Sobs: "Hated me, even."

"But she was your mom," I say. It feels like a stupid thing to have said, but it is so hard to watch my dad sitting there, his face wet with tears and snot, like a little boy.

"It was hard for her, Kassidy." He sniffs and then wipes his whole face with his sleeve, looks at how gross it is now, and hides it under the table. "She loved my dad and, try as I might, I was nothing like him. Nothing I ever did was good enough. When I was sixteen—the day after my birthday, it was—she kicked me out. 'Take your stuff, and don't come back until you've made something of yourself. Make your dad proud.' She said I'd thank her one day."

He goes quiet and stares into space. But I can't let him stop now.

"And did you? Thank her?" I'm trying not to let it show in my voice that I think his mom sounds horrible.

He gets up and walks to the sink.

"Didn't have the chance, Kassidy."

"Oh."

He's hunched over.

"How did she die?" I say, because I can't think what else to do except ask stupid questions.

"She didn't," he says, standing up straight and looking back at me briefly. "I went back five years later and she'd gone. Moved, I mean. No address. No message."

"Well, maybe she tried to contact you but she couldn't find you, Dad. Maybe—"

"No, Kassidy," he says firmly. "I think I knew, even that first day I left, that I'd never see her again. She wanted to be rid of me. I wasn't good enough. She's still out there, Kassidy, not wanting to know me because I'm . . . still . . . nothing."

"Dad! Don't say that!"

"It's OK, Kassidy—I'm OK. I'll drag myself back up— always do. I'm just thinking out loud."

I wish I knew what to do. Suddenly this huge chunk of Dad's history is here in the room, and it explains so much, but it's too big to take in.

"Forty, Kass. I'm nearly forty. And what have I got to show for it?"

I open my mouth to defend him and his life, but I think he's going to answer it himself, looking out the window into the neat square garden, or more likely looking at his own reflection in the glass.

"I've got two wonderful children. And I *did* have a wonderful wife. But I ruined that, too."

"No, Dad, that's not fair." I get up and go to him, try to wrap my arms around him from the side.

"What should I do, Kassidy?" He looks me in the eye.

"Come home, Dad."

✳ *Chapter Twenty-five* ✳

Two Sandwiches Short of a Picnic

This is me, imagining my parents arguing at the kitchen table: still round, still with the red vinyl apples, only everything else is different now.

This is me; this is how I am. It is Saturday night but there's no pizza—who'd have thought I'd ever miss that painful little ritual? I'm in my bedroom with a family bag of Cheetos, a bottle of Sprite, and four chocolate-covered graham crackers (Mom's been guilt-shopping again). It's OK, I'm going to take up running soon. Preferably far away from this place.

Joke.

There's an irritating smooshing against the door. I'm secretly glad it's Raff but I can't let the team down (the team being all bad-tempered older sisters everywhere, holla!), so I say, "What?" It's not really a question, but an expression of how unwelcome he is.

"I'm hungry. You've got all the food," he says. I try to lick the evidence off my fingers but they are stained orange.

"OK, come in."

Raff lies stomach-down on my bed and puts an entire chocolate-covered graham cracker in his mouth.

"That's gross," I say. His reply is very crumby. Then he puts his chocolaty mouth on the Sprite bottle and glugs. I make the appropriate face. It's difficult to believe that this model of sophistication, now belching loudly, is the same one who almost got mixed up in a gang. Bless him, poor little guy. He still carries his BlackBerry everywhere, and seems to have more money than any thirteen-year-old should. But I know he's OK. We talk now.

"What are they arguing about?" I say.

"Dad put an empty milk carton back in the fridge."

"Are you kidding?"

"Uh, *yes*. What do you *think* they're arguing about, Kass? Dumb question."

Oh. It's nice that I have taught my little brother one thing: sarcasm.

"But what specifically?" I say.

"He's asking her what your friend's dad's got that he doesn't."

"And what's she saying?"

"Paul, can't we just talk about us instead of him? That's over."

"Is that supposed to be an impression of Mom? That sucks."

"Whatever. Can I have another cookie?"

I hand him one and wipe the Sprite bottle with my sleeve before taking a swig.

"So, what's happening with you?" I ask. He shrugs. "Raff,

if you're going to spend the evening in my room you have to actually talk to me."

"All right. Umm . . . I got picked for the soccer team."

"Yeah? That's fabulous. Did you tell Dad?"

"Yep."

"What did he say?"

"He said good."

"OK. Good."

"Yep." He pretends not to be too bothered, but I know different now, and I've got to do my part to get them closer together. "Hey, Kass, remember that time I blacked out the TV screen with permanent marker and told Mom and Dad it was you?"

"Raff, are you going to make a long list of confessions now that I've helped you out and you like me again? Because I've got a long memory." I smile at him.

"Just that one. Sorry." He's smiling, too. Idiot. Lovable idiot.

"What else is happening?"

"Umm . . . I dunno. When are we doing that family therapy stuff?"

"Next week."

"Is it gonna be weird? I don't want to do anything weird."

"I think she's just going to lock us in a tiny room and release hundreds of spiders into it."

"*What?*"

For a smart little boy he sure is gullible.

"Joke. It's just going to be talking and stuff. *Feeeeelings*. You know those? I think you've got one somewhere, buried deep, deep down."

He turns the Cheetos bag upside down over his mouth and gets orange dust in his eyes. When he's restored his vision he says: "Are we gonna have to talk about *Graham*?" He says *Graham* with a fairly decent robot voice and does robot hands to go with it.

"Maybe. They're moving, you know. Him and Char. Izzy told me."

"Oh, right. Hey, have you finished the cookies?"

Brothers.

Raff starts to listen to my iPod, making a face every time he flicks to a new song. Then his face relaxes and he flips onto his back. It's sort of nice to have him here, even if he's no good at gossip and hasn't noticed that he has a blob of chocolate on the end of his nose.

I go online. Stix isn't IM'ing, and that's probably a good thing. He's sent me a few nice texts but I'm trying to keep my distance until all the fuzzy feelings are gone. Then *maybe* we can be friends. He messed up that night but I'm OK; it's not the end of everything. It's getting easier to think that he's a good guy who made a mistake. Confession: There's even a tiny part of me that wonders if we could ever be more than friends. But where do you go when the beginning of a relationship is so difficult? Maybe if you've been together for years, and your life together is so tangled up, you can move past it—like Mom and Dad say they're trying to—but I'm too young to compromise.

The only person online is Char. We haven't spoken since the clarinet lesson, except for the time that Mom and I had to drag Dad away from her front door and she said coldly: "Just go." And I replied, "Sorry," and held back my sobbing father while he promised to do all sorts of violent things to *Graham*.

I should think of what I want to say before I type a word, but that might make me lose my nerve.

curlygirl: hello, do u want to talk?

char: about what?

curlygirl: how sorry i am?

char: how sorry are you?

curlygirl: big-time. i never meant to hurt u

char: i know

curlygirl: i did kiss him at first. i shouldn't have. and then it got scary. it was my fault i'm really sorry

char: izzy told me everything. not xactly a dream boy, was he? i'm sorry too

curlygirl: u r? what for?

char: being a total nut job. it wasn't so much about that. well it was and it wasn't.

curlygirl: yeah i know. what i don't get is why u didn't tell me what was going on.

. . .

curlygirl: char?

char: yep, well, that's the screwed-up part. the whole reason I found out was because dad had stopped grounding me for having a hair out of place etc. etc. he seemed happy and I got suspicious. overheard him on phone.

curlygirl: no way—that's how i found out. god, aren't they idiots?

char: tmai. so anyway half of me was like totally furious and the other half didn't want dad to get hurt again like he did when my mom left. she was—your mom, I mean—a really good influence on him.

I sit back in my chair and look at those words: *a really good influence.* I don't think I've ever known Mom to influence Dad until recently; in fact, that's what used to make me so angry.

curlygirl: that's weird. 2 b honest don't really want to think about it anymore

char: me neither

. . .

char: our place is up for sale

curlygirl: yeah i know

char: but we're not moving that far away after all. Dad doesn't want me to switch schools with SATs next year. He asked me what I thought about going to school with u and stuff—the first time he's ever asked me what I thought.

curlygirl: well?

char: well what?

curlygirl: well what do u think about going to school with me?

. . .

curlygirl: if u could answer a tad quicker that would really help how sick and nervous i feel over here!!

char: guess it'll be weird. doesn't feel weird on here tho

curlygirl: yeah I know. maybe we start with IM and slowly build up to IRL conversation

char: sounds good

curlygirl: ☺ better not tell my dad tho. he's really messed up about evrythng. but we're going to fam therapy. we've been izzy-fied ☺

char: think i might avoid telling mine too

curlygirl: hey we'll be like romeo and juliet

char: omg don't remind me, haven't even started my essay!!

curlygirl: rebel

char: ☺

curlygirl: ☺

It's about midnight and there's dribble on my pillow—Raff has dozed off. It might be the stress of my home life, or the amount of additives I've consumed this evening, but I'm not even close to tired so I tiptoe downstairs for a change of scene and more supplies.

On the way down I hear Dad snoring in their bedroom. (I think it's still accurate to refer to it as theirs.) It's good that he's asleep—since Mom confessed, the whole time he's awake it's painful to watch him. He swings from horrible, sad self-deprecation to unbelievable meanness, then regret, then cringe-inducing showiness, all in the space of five minutes, while Mom stands by totally dignified. A few weeks ago I'd have thought she was being cold and unfeeling, but now I know that this is just the only way to deal with Dad—let him go through it all until he comes out the other side. Hopefully once we've gone to therapy a few times we'll find out new ways of coping. The strangest thing is, even with all this going on, he hasn't gone back to Planet Down—it's weird how it hasn't sent him over the edge. I guess it's not in our control after all. It really is those nameless chemicals and not some rational thing we can contain.

The new duvet is crumpled on the sofa. Every morning Mom hides it away before we get up, as if we're that stupid. It seems weird that she'd want to protect us from the fact that they're sleeping in different rooms when we already know what happened and Dad mentions it approximately seven times an hour.

It sounds like she's unpacking the dishwasher.

"Hi," I say from the doorway.

"Oh, hi, Kass. I thought you'd be asleep."

"I was hungry."

I take an apple from the fruit bowl—surely that cancels out at least one cookie—and sit at the table. This is the first time we've been alone since the night of the disco; not that she hasn't tried to make it happen before, but I haven't let her. I'm not saying I've forgiven her now—I still feel like she betrayed me and Raff as well as Dad—but I understand her better. It wasn't just her. It didn't happen because my mom's horrible.

I hope everyone knows how wise I am these days. Ha. Izzy would be proud, though she's been busy lately with her dysfunctional-turned-sweetheart parents and her new therapist. She decided she needed a new one. I don't really know how it all works, but I guess I'll find out.

Strange: I've been so scared of losing everything—and of Dad losing IT—that I've barely realized what I've gained. I've gotten my little brother back and it feels like I could have Mom back, too. In a new and better way. That's why I'm sitting here, I guess, watching her clean the kitchen, watching her stay the course instead of cracking up, watching her and wondering how I never really saw her before.

"I'm making tea," she says. I expect she doesn't ask whether I want any because the last time she asked I told her to stick her tea up her . . .

"Yes, please," I say.

✳ *Chapter Twenty-six* ✳

I Have a Dream, a Song to Sing

(ONE YEAR LATER)

Here I am, Kass Kennedy, one in a million—that is, one average-looking, tone-deaf girl in a line of a million people waiting to audition for *The X Factor*. Yes! Me! OK, so a million might be a slight exaggeration—a year later I'm still no better at Math. I even doodled my brain falling out of my head on my midterm. Dad would be so proud.

He doesn't know I'm here. I thought about telling him, but he's not ready for it yet. He's come a long way, my dad, but it would be the equivalent of blowing cigarette smoke in his face and crowing *nah-nah-nah-nah-nah* (he gave those up, too—I can't say which was harder for him but at least you can buy nicotine patches; he had to go cold turkey on the pushy parent stuff).

Let's get one thing straight: I'm not here because I think I've got the X factor. As if! I'm still just normal, ordinary Kass. Doing this is symbolic. I don't even care how stupid that sounds. Maybe I'm high on audition-line fumes: the heady pollution of all these hopefuls, and knowing that I can enjoy this for what it is. I have zero expectations.

We're passing the time by having a heated debate about what to sing. We're *that* prepared.

"OK, so we've narrowed it down to 'Dancing Queen' or 'Girls Just Want to Have Fun,'" I say. "*Or* the weird song that Izzy's boyfriend wrote for her." I know I'm being a smart-ass, but I also know I can be with my best friends.

"It's not *weird*," says Izzy. "Is it, Char?"

"*Weird* is a bit strong; we just don't know it, Izz, that's all. It's a great song, but maybe not for today." Sometimes it's really hard to believe that Char was ever *not* this nice. Izzy's boyfriend is a metalhead and the "love song" he wrote her sounds like someone having their tonsils removed without anesthetic, and contains the phrases *I am your slave* and *Come to my lair through the catacombs*. Cute.

"Fine," says Izzy, "but we're not singing 'Dancing Queen'—it's a well-known fact that no one can sing that except ABBA. It's physically impossible, even for good singers."

"True, but do we care?" says Char. "You want to be a therapist, I want to be a doctor, and Kass wants to have a column in a magazine where she can bitch about life in a *very* sarcastic manner. None of us actually wants to pass the audition. Right, Kass?"

"Right, but I really, really want to audition in front of Simon," I say. "So we need to pass this first part or we won't get to meet him."

"What is it with you and Simon Cowell? Do you have an old-man crush on him or what?" says Izzy.

"Oh, yeah, totally. Not. Anyway, if I wanted someone who looked like him I could just get it on with my dad's best friend."

"Eww, Furby, that's gross. Is your dad *still* trying to launch Tony whatshisname?"

"Ferrari. Yep. He's even set up this new company called Looky Likey. Tony's his only client so far. It's a bit sad, but you know my dad. At least I'm not on his client list. Anyway, they're great friends. Like brothers. It's kind of sweet."

"Aww, yeah, it is sweet," says Char.

"Interesting," says Izzy, probably jotting it down in her imaginary therapist's notebook.

"I just . . . I really *like* Simon Cowell," I say, as if this is news even to me. "And I want to do this one crazy thing to mark the end of our exams and the fact that we're all still best friends even though . . . *you know*, there was all the weird stuff but now it's all cool and . . . OK, am I getting too mushy?"

"Mushy's good," says Char. "Although by the looks of this line we have about a month to decide what to sing. I can't believe how many people are here. Hey, do you know whether, um, Cassian and his band are coming this year?"

This is progress. It took Char and me about six months to stop referring to Cass as "him." More recently he's been upgraded to "um, Cassian." Not that we talk about him much, but somehow he and I managed to stay friends—the kind of friend you don't speak to all the time, but when you do it feels like you never stopped. Who'd have thought?

"Didn't Simon Cowell call him 'smelly and tone-deaf' last year?" says Izzy.

"I think it was 'greasy and distinctly average,' actually," I say. "Anyway, he's busy at college and playing weekend gigs."

"You still hear from him, then." Izzy's voice is flat and deeply disapproving. She wouldn't give Cass the time of day if he saved her from a burning building, out of loyalty to me. I love her for it; I'd be the same if it had happened to her. "Doesn't Joe mind?"

Joe . . . Joe . . . rings a vague bell. OK, OK, Joe's my boyfriend. This is all a bit new, so excuse me if I blush several shades of scarlet, wear a dumb grin, and start giggling. It's not my fault!

"Joe is absolutely fine with it," I say, using every muscle in my face not to beam at my interrogator. The girls both go *awwww* and rub my arms as if I'm a playful puppy. *Ahem, pull yourself together, Kass!*

"OK, back to business. The audition: the reason we're standing here in this ridiculous line. The way I see it, we either have to be unbelievably bad—which actually requires some skill if you check out some of the people here—or we have to be halfway good, which we could be if Izzy and I sing like mice and you really belt it out, Char."

271

"Hmm, I'll do my best, Furbs," she says. (Did I also fail to mention that use of the nickname had spread like an evil virus?) "And if Izzy flashes some leg, and you make a few biting remarks, we might actually do it."

So we decide on "Girls Just Want to Have Fun." We huddle together and sing into the top of our bottles of water. I can't say I feel relaxed, but this nervous, cloud-nine buzz is just from the thought of laying all this to rest, finally, and because I'm with my best friends, who know everything about me and still, somehow, want to stick around.

We did it.

I'm so excited, a really tiny part of me wants to call my dad and tell him I passed the first stage, but that would be cruel, and I don't need his approval on this—that's not what this is about.

"I can't believe they put us through," says Char.

"I know. Are we so bad we're good, or so good we don't know it?" says Izzy.

"I don't care. This is amazing," I say. They both look at me and smile. I feel really young and silly, and good about that.

People are coming out of the judges' room crying, and we've made a pact never to make a joke about them. But everyone else is open to abuse (quietly). And to be fair, we also make jokes about each other in between.

"What about him?" whispers Izzy. "Looks like he ironed his jeans. Isn't that illegal?"

"My dad used to iron his," I say. "But he's been rehabilitated now. Ooh, look at her with the tramp stamp and the yellow thong."

"Nasty," says Char. "Wait—look at *him*."

"Yeah, he's nice," I say. And we look at each other. "You have him."

"Nah."

"What do you mean, nah? He's hot!"

Char shrugs and tries to hide a smile.

"Charlotte, you tell me this minute what that smile is about!"

"I have absolutely no idea what you . . . OK! But you promise not to laugh?"

"Cross our hearts," says Izzy, and we both clamp our hands over our mouths.

"OK. There's a new family on our street and one of the boys is really, really cute. New Dream Boy!"

"You're kidding—what is it about the streets where you live? It's like wherever you move, the universe gives you a hot guy as a housewarming gift!" I say. "So, does Dream Boy have a name?"

Char swanks around a bit and then says:

"He has a name, a phone number, and a date next week!"

The three of us squeal like guinea pigs until a voice says: "30786."

My heart skips a beat.

"That's us," I say. "I can't do it."

"30786?"

"Oh, yes, you can, Furbs," says Izzy. "You're brave. You're brilliant."

"We're with you, Kass," says Char.

"30786? Are you 30786?" says a frazzled girl with a clipboard.

"Yes," I say. I stand up; my legs are like jelly. "That's us."

"Come this way, please, girls. Simon is waiting."

AUTHOR'S NOTE

All the characters and events in this book are imagined, but my decision to write about how mental health can shape lives comes from real experiences. Stories passed down through several generations of my family have made me think deeply about how much prejudice and misconception still exists about mental health, and about how the mental illness of a parent could affect a family.

When someone is suffering, we look for reasons why. A family member or close friend who has a mental illness can make us wonder, like Kass wonders, *Did I cause this?* Or equally, *Will this happen to me?* It can be very lonely, scary, and stressful, but you don't have to go through it alone. Help is out there.

In the United States, about 1 in 4 adults will suffer from a diagnosable mental disorder in any given year. If you are worried about someone close, or about yourself, talking is the first important step. Ask your family doctor, your school guidance counselor or health education teacher, or another trusted adult for advice. The National Institute for Mental Health's website, *www.nimh.nih.gov*, also has helpful information and resources about who you can talk to and what you can do. Take care.

ABOUT THE AUTHOR

Emily Gale currently lives in Melbourne, Australia, with her partner, children, and cats; she works as a reader for a literary agent. Before that she was a freelance writer in London, publishing a fictional magazine column and several picture books, including *Doctor Pig* and the Just Josie series. This was not long after she became a mom and then wandered about in a daze for months, wondering just what she'd got herself into. Before that she was slightly more glamorous (well, she wore heels and makeup, at least) working as an editor, mainly of children's books — "the Peter Rabbit Years," she refers to them mysteriously. This was preceded by her studying English at the University of Sussex, where she developed a taste for editing by working on student magazines. She also developed a taste for taking a midnight dip in the English Channel. Pre-university she was a part-time groupie who was always falling in love with guitar-playing, long-haired boys. As a schoolgirl in lurid purple uniform she studied hard by day and wrote toe-curlingly bad poetry by night, any evidence of which is now safely buried in a lockbox on a tiny archipelago in the southern Indian Ocean. Her toddler years are marked by the nickname "Kojak," because, like that bald TV detective from the seventies, she didn't have any hair. She did have a temper, though, and didn't speak to her mother for two whole weeks when her baby brother was brought home from the hospital. And before any of this happened she was born on a snowy day in London, in 1975, and the possibilities were endless.

ACKNOWLEDGMENTS

In this book are more than just my own fingerprints. All the interesting changes made to create this American edition are the work of Siobhán McGowan, with help from Starr Baer, and I'd like to thank them for their sensitivity and attention to detail, and for making this such an enjoyable process. My grateful acknowledgment also, and in particular, to: my agent, Louise Burns; my editor, Imogen Cooper; my friend Caroline Green; and the Anonymous Reader at Hilary Johnson's Author's Advisory Service, for their wonderful insights.

Thank you to the very talented team at Chicken House, the wits at MsB, and those at WW who gave great feedback. Thank you to Sascha, Ruth, and Kellie for true friendship, and to Dan Box for timely kicks up the rear. Thanks to my supportive parents, Sue and Chris Gale. And finally, thank you to Aaron, for always knowing when I need to go back to the Shire.